MARY CRAWFORD

THE *Heart* OF *Summers*

HIDDEN BEAUTY BOOK 13

COPYRIGHT

Published on December 11, 2019, by Diversity Ink Press and Mary Crawford. Author may be reached at MaryCrawfordAuthor.com.

ISBN-978-1-945637-61-2 • ASIN: B081ZVG2M3

Cover by Covers Unbound

Hidden Beauty Series

Until the Stars Fall from the Sky

So the Heart Can Dance

Joy and Tiers

Love Naturally

Love Seasoned

Love Claimed

If You Knew Me (and other silent musings) (novella)

Jude's Song

The Price of Freedom (novella)

Paths Not Taken

Dreams Change (novella)

Heart Wish

Tempting Fate

The Letter

The Power of Will

HIDDEN HEARTS SERIES

Identity of the Heart
Sheltered Hearts
Hearts of Jade
Port in the Storm (novella)
Love is More Than Skin Deep
Tough
Rectify
Pieces (a crossover novel)
Hearts Set Free
Freedom (a crossover novel)
The Long Road to Love (novella)

HIDDEN HEARTS - PROTECTION UNIT
Love and Injustice
Out of Thin Air
Soul Scars

OTHER WORKS:
The Power of Dictation
An Everyday Guide to Scrivener 3 for Mac
An Everyday Guide to Scrivener 3 for Windows
Vision of the Heart

DEDICATION

To all the parents who
struggle every day to
celebrate the child
they were given
and not mourn
the one they hoped for.

CHAPTER ONE

JOE

I GRIT MY TEETH as Brody plays a song with a cartoon dinosaur singing off-key for what seems like the billionth time. I know these shows are educational, but sometimes I wonder if it's worth the pain to my ears.

As I pick up my guitar and start to play Aidan O'Brien's new song, Brody abruptly stands up and starts twirling.

I look up. "What's wrong, Brod?" Even after all these years, I still reflexively ask questions like that — although I know he's never going to answer me.

He stands on his tiptoes and walks over to the kitchen. I cringe as he starts digging through a paper bag full of things to recycle. Darn it, I should have remembered to take it out to the trash bins.

I flip my guitar case open with my foot and prepare to put my guitar, Janis, in it. Suddenly, Brody walks around the corner holding a grocery receipt and a used container of yogurt.

"Oh, you're hungry. You want a grilled cheese sandwich?"

Brody shakes his head so hard it must make him dizzy. He holds the receipt out to me and then shoves the yogurt container in my face.

I take a deep breath and let it out. This would be so much easier if autism didn't rob my beautiful child of his speech. Or, that's what some doctors think. Some seem to believe Brody is selectively mute. Still others have mumbled under their breath about Munchausen's Syndrome by Proxy.

As I'm thinking, Brody slaps the receipt against my cheek. The movement is so abrupt I jump. Then he pulls my hand from my guitar and stuffs the receipt in it. I take a moment to glance at it. The side of my mouth quirks up. Sure enough, there's strawberry yogurt, goldfish crackers, and chocolate milk on the list.

"So, let me guess … We have a refrigerator full of food but nothing you want to eat?"

Brody spins around and walks to the front door, takes his coat off the rack, and puts it on.

I set Janis down in the guitar case and close it. Rubbing my temples, I respond, "The grocery store it is. I guess I wasn't getting much accomplished here anyway."

Brody stares at me blankly, but walks over to the kitchen table and grabs my car keys from the wooden bowl in the center. He stands on his tiptoes and twirls around before he hands them to me.

"Just a second, buddy. I have to turn off the TV and call my boss."

I stuff the keys in my pocket and pull out my cell phone. With my thumb, I call Aidan. To my surprise, he answers on the first ring.

"Uh … I thought you were going out to dinner with Maddie and Tara," I stammer. "I was planning to leave you a message."

"I would be, except the ramp on the van is busted. Maddie and Tara are at the repair shop trying to get it fixed. They got stranded at the store."

"I'm sorry. I have kid issues. So I called to let you know I wouldn't be at the jam session tonight. Brody wants to go to the store."

"He told you that?" Aidan's voice raises in surprise.

I sigh. "Yeah, I guess you could say that. He's making his intentions clear, anyway."

"Gotcha. We'll miss you tonight. I'm not worried, you are the consummate professional. I'm sure you'll have the new playlist memorized by the time we go out on tour."

The pounding behind my left eye suddenly becomes intense. "I hope so. It's probably a good thing I'm not coming tonight. This sinus thing is killing me. Who gets a stupid cold in the middle of summer?"

"Happens to me all the time, Joe. Summer colds are the pits. Take care. The world needs you healthy," Aidan says as I hear his phone click. "Gotta go. I think Tara is calling."

"Talk to you later. I need to go too. Brody is getting impatient."

Brody's practically dragging me down the dairy aisle. This is the third time we've traversed the aisle. He is frantically looking at every type of yogurt and pudding snack available.

I squat down to talk to him, "There doesn't seem to be any strawberry left. Do you want cherry or lemon?"

Brody covers his ears and sits on the floor in front of the case. When I reach for him, he curls up in a ball and tears stream down his face. People are staring at us and shaking their heads as they edge their carts past us. He still has the black eye he received from running into his trampoline while he was playing fetch with Scout. I'm sure it looks like I have been beating the snot out of him.

A woman approaches, and I steel myself for a barrage of criticism. My head feels like it's going to explode. I guess I should go to the doctor. When the heck am I going to find the time?

Brody's eyes widen when he sees the woman stop in front of us. Honestly, mine do too. The woman looks like she is stuck in the 60s. Her long legs are encased in white go-go boots, and she's wearing a lime green, electric orange and hot pink miniskirt. Her shirt is a bright orange turtleneck with tassels on the sleeves. She's wearing big hoop earrings.

Rather than talk down to me, she squats next to me and studies Brody as he hugs his knees and continues to cry silently.

She turns to me and whispers, "Is he okay?"

I don't know whether to weep or laugh at her innocent inquiry. She has no idea how loaded her question is. I nod. "They're out of strawberry yogurt."

She stands up and reaches over the top of Brody's head to grab some strawberry yogurt. She squats down and tries to look Brody in the eye. "Here you go. I've had this kind before, it's yummy!"

Brody shakes his head and starts to tremble. I reach out to touch his shoulder as I look up at the hopeful stranger. "Thank you for your help. Brody is kind of particular about yogurt." I reach down and try to grasp his hand. "Come on, Buddy, let's go to a different store and see if we can find it."

Brody pulls away from me as he digs in my jacket pocket and retrieves the receipt I stuffed in there earlier. I'm completely gobsmacked when he holds it up to the woman with the wild clothes.

She glances over at me. "You mind?"

I try to cover my tears as I shake my head. She can't possibly know she's just witnessed a miracle. Brody doesn't spontaneously interact with anyone except me, his dog, his therapist, and his teacher.

She takes the crumpled receipt from his hand. "Thank you, Brody. Did you know I have a B name too? It kind of rhymes with yours. My name is Brynley."

Brody just stares at her.

Brynley shrugs. "I guess you must be shy. That's okay, I understand." She smooths out the receipt and looks at it. "Oh, you must like chocolate milk. I love it too. I am supposed to be a grown-up, but I like to eat chocolate milk on my Cocoa Puffs. Everyone thinks I'm weird."

I grin. "Actually, it sounds pretty good. Add some coffee to your breakfast menu, and you would be buzzing all day. Brody doesn't talk to anyone, so don't take it personally."

Faster than I can blink, Brynley is on her knees in front of Brody. "Hi, my name is B-R-Y-N-L-E-Y," she signs with exacting precision as she finger-spells her name.

I'm about to interrupt her to let her know Brody can hear her just fine when I see him beam a wide smile at her. I have to turn away as tears fill my eyes. I live to see that smile and Brynley, a perfect stranger, was able to elicit it by just telling him her name. I don't know if I should rejoice or bawl like a baby.

I feel someone touch my thigh. Jolted back to reality, I glance over at my son and notice Brynley studying me intently.

"Are you okay?" she whispers softly. "Can I help?"

Talk about a loaded question. I clear my throat. "I'll survive. It's just been a tough day. I'm not sure if you can help."

She rolls her shoulder. "I'm sorry if I'm overstepping my bounds, but I'm here if you need me." She turns to Brody. She signs as she speaks. I know some basic sign language having worked with Aidan O'Brien for several years, but her fingers are flying too fast for me to follow, so I'm grateful that she's speaking too. "Brody, I'm sorry they don't have your favorite yogurt. I want to show you something if that's okay. Your dad can come with us, but it's in another aisle."

Brynley stands up and reaches her hand out for Brody. Much to my shock, he places his hand in hers as if he did it every day of the week. His behavior therapist and I have been working on that skill for years since he has a tendency to dart into traffic.

Brynley looks over her shoulder. "You coming?"

Brody makes a motion with his head to indicate I should follow them. Mutely, I do.

I watch in stunned amazement as Brynley walks down the aisle hand-in-hand with my son.

When a cart gets too close to Brody, she lets go of his hand and puts her arm protectively around his shoulders. When I do that, Brody tends to freeze. Yet, there they are strolling down the aisle as if nothing out of the ordinary just happened.

Suddenly, Brynley smiles and reaches out to pick something up off the shelf. "Oh, here it is. I don't know why they don't keep this with the rest of the yogurts. I guess it's because it's organic or something. All I can tell you is it's the best thing I've ever put in my mouth. It's like eating hot chocolate! What do you say, Brody? You think you can try this instead of the strawberry?"

You could have knocked me over with a feather when Brody takes it from her hand and puts it in our basket.

"Cool beans! I hope you like it as much as I do. You want to see the crackers I like almost as much as goldfish?" Brynley asks as she winks at me. The mischievous look on her face is mesmerizing. I don't know why I didn't notice before, but she is enchanting.

Distracted by her beauty, it takes me a bit to find my voice. "I'd like to know. Sometimes, goldfish can be monotonous."

Brody grabs Brynley's hand and then escorts her back to me, where he tries to grab my hand. I adjust my hold on the shopping basket and join the happy little parade in search of the mysterious crackers.

When we reach the cracker aisle, Brynley slows down and examines the boxes. "Here they are, and they're even on sale! It's our lucky day." She pulls a box off the shelf and shows it to Brody. "I know they look a little funny because they have a chicken on the front of them — but they are the total bomb. I especially like them if I'm eating chicken soup. When I was little, my grandma had these at her house."

Brody looks at me quizzically.

I chuckle. "Yeah, I used to eat these as a kid too. I totally forgot about them, but I used to love them. You want some?"

Brody lets go of my hand and takes the box of crackers from Brynley and puts it in the basket.

"Great! Would you like to get some soup to go with those crackers?" Brynley asks with a huge grin.

Brody looks to me for permission. "If that's what you want, go for it."

Brody grabs my hand and then Brynley's before we go on a hunt for chicken soup. I take a deep breath and blow it out. It wasn't a one-time fluke — he deliberately reached out to her again.

As we're making our way down the aisle, we have to move over to avoid colliding with an endcap of snack foods. Brody stops and picks up a box. He holds it up for Brynley to see.

"I love those. The strawberry flavor is awesome! I used to try to peel them off the back in tiny bites to make them last as long as I could," Brynley replies.

Brody nods imperceptibly as he places the rollups in our shopping basket. Then, he walks over and grabs Brynley's hand again.

"You know, that's a really good idea." Brynley picks up a box.

"Would you like to put it in our basket? Your hands are a little busy." I offer.

She shrugs. "Sure, we'll probably be checking out at the same time anyway." She looks down at Brody. "Let's go see if we can find the soup. I like the soup from the deli here."

Together, we traipse through the store hand-in-hand. Strangers looking at us would never guess I don't even know Brynley's last name. We look like a quintessential modern family with Brody skipping between us.

Brody stops dead in his tracks when he sees the soup kiosk. He's such a picky eater, it never occurred to me to show him this option before.

Brynley grins. "I know! It's amazing, isn't it? I love to come here just to smell the soup cooking. It reminds me of my grandma's house. She used to make it all the time. Do you want a big bowl or a small bowl? Personally, I like to get the big one, so I have leftovers." She lowers her voice down to a whisper. "Sometimes, I can't decide which flavor I like best, so I get two kinds."

Brody looks up at me with a questioning gaze. "Get what you want," I instruct, still not believing the scene unfolding in front of me.

Brynley picks Brody up and hitches him on her hip so he can see inside the kettles of soup. "See this green one? It looks gross, but it tastes really good. It's split pea. The one with the tortilla shells on it is Mexican tomato soup, but it's too spicy for me. I tried it once and had to go find some milk to drink. Look! They have chicken soup. The noodles in the chicken soup taste like they are homemade."

Brynley pauses to take a breath and Brody points at the last kettle.

"Oh, you're right. I missed one," Brynley continues as if she's having a full-on conversation with Brody. "This one has little tiny noodles that look like shells. It's minestrone. I love this one because it smells so good."

"I don't know if he'll eat something like —" I start to say before Brody helps himself to one of the bowls and points to the minestrone soup.

"Excellent choice. Is that the size you want?" Brynley asks as she eyes the large bowl.

"That's fine. Whatever he doesn't eat, I can."

Brynley fills up the bowl and hands it to me before she asks, "Anything else?"

Brody lets go of my hand and runs over to the other side of me to pick up the box of crackers. He points to the chicken on the front of the box.

"Chicken soup it is! I think you'll love this one," Brynley signs as she replies.

Brody grins when he sees her sign for chicken.

"Oh, you like that? This means chicken," she exclaims as she makes a gesture in front of her mouth and then pecks the palm of her other hand.

Shyly, Brody puts his fingers up in front of his nose and mimics her.

"Perfect! You have excellent sign language skills," Brynley gushes as she gives my son a high five. As she turns to fill the bowl with chicken soup, I sway a little on my feet as the blood rushes from my head.

Brody notices my odd movement and pulls on one of the tassels on Brynley's shirt sleeves as he points to me.

Brynley gasps when she sees me. "My gosh, are you hurt? You look pale as a ghost."

"It's been an unusual day. To be honest with you, I don't feel so well."

CHAPTER TWO

BRYNLEY

I JUST CAME TO pick up some ice cream, chicken strips, and JoJos. Now, this guy looks like he's about to pass out. I frantically look around the store. Finally, I find one of those blood pressure machines. There's a chair next to it. I hand Brody the basket of groceries. "Is this too heavy for you? I need to help your dad."

I think Brody shakes his head. But I can't really tell. I don't even know this guy's name. Still, he obviously needs help, and helping people is what I do. I slide my arm around his waist and motion for Brody to follow me as I escort his father to a safer location. I don't usually feel dwarfed by men, but this man is a tall drink of water.

Finally, we reach the orange plastic chair, and I help the guy sit down. As soon as I do, Brody starts to twirl and flap his hands. Suddenly, things start to make a little more sense. Of all the things I thought I would use my special ed minor for, a trip to the grocery store wasn't one of them.

"Brody, look. Your dad is resting in a chair. It's going to be okay."

After a couple of minutes, Brody stops and looks at me. Reflexively, I reach out to brush some hair out of his dad's face. "Oh geez! He's burning up," I blurt before I consider the ramifications. "I don't even know who he is."

Brody shrugs off his backpack and hands me a laminated, bright orange card.

I breathe a sigh of relief. Okay, at least now I have a name: Joseph Summers. Why does his name sound so familiar? I'm sure I would've remembered meeting the tall, blonde guy with the lumberjack good looks.

I turn the card over and over in my hand as I try to formulate a plan which won't upset Brody. "I don't suppose you have a phone in that magic backpack of yours, do you?"

Brody is statue-still for a few moments. Then, he sets his backpack down on the ground and walks over to Joseph, who appears to be sleeping. Gently, Brody opens his jacket and pulls out a cell phone. He hands it to me and watches me carefully.

The picture on the lock screen is an adorable candid shot of Brody and some sort of Terrier mix. Okay, that's good, it's definitely the right phone. Crap! He's got a screen lock on his phone.

"Don't suppose you know the code?" I ask Brody with a raised eyebrow. I glance over to Joseph as he shifts in the chair trying to make his long frame comfortable.

Brody takes the phone from me and punches in some numbers before he hands it back. "I'm so lucky you're smart," I mumble to myself.

I thumb through his contacts. There are several female names in his phone. Vaguely, I wonder if he's a player.

"Brody, which one is your mom?"

He shrugs and starts to bounce on his tiptoes.

"Umm …Okay, time for plan B. I guess I'll dial the last number he called. Maybe it's your mom."

I press redial on Joseph's phone and hope for the best.

When the phone connects, the name that pops up is Bossman. Before I can process that, a voice answers. "Joe, my man. You have the worst timing. Maddie is in the tub. What's up?"

"Uh, hi. This isn't Joe. This is Brynley. I'm at the grocery store with your friend Joe and his son. He isn't feeling well. I'm not sure what to do."

"Is he okay? What happened? I just talked to him a while ago —" the voice demands.

"I don't know. We were picking out soup for Brody to eat for dinner, and your friend looked a little peaked, as my grandma would say. I'm not sure what's going on, but he's burning up."

"How is Brody dealing with this? Is he safe?"

"It's hard to tell, but he seems okay. He's clutching my hand right now, but he's not crying."

"Brody is touching you?" The person sounds incredulous.

"Yeah … Is that a big deal? He and I are buddies. We bonded over missing yogurt."

"That makes me feel better. How long have you known Brody?"

I cringe as I glance at the time on Joseph's cell phone. "Oh, I'd say about forty-five minutes," I answer, feeling like an idiot.

"Who am I talking to?" The voice on the other end

of the phone demands.

I clear my throat. "I'm Brynley Meeker. Don't worry, Brody is safe with me. I work for Locate My Heart and I love kids. I'm just trying to make sure I don't need to call an ambulance for your friend or something."

I hear the person on the other end of the phone heave a sigh. "Thank heavens! Hi Brynley, I don't know if you remember me from Kendall's benefit. But this is Aidan O'Brien."

I almost drop the phone. "Aidan O'Brien, like *the* Aidan O'Brien? Top of iTunes and Grammy winner, Aidan O'Brien?"

"I take it you've heard of me?" Aidan says with a smile in his voice.

I groan. "I knew this guy looked familiar. Joe Summers, your acoustic guitar player, is sprawled out on the chair in front of me. He looks really sick. I don't think chicken soup is going to fix him."

"Where are you guys?" Aidan asks.

"I think the store is called CJ's Market. I just come here because I like the food in their deli. Brody was having a tough time, so I tried to make him feel better."

"I'm glad you did that. Hang tight. I'll send one of the guys from my security detail to help you guys out."

I swallow hard. "Not trying to tell you how to handle your business or anything, but I don't think anybody's going to hurt Joe. I think he needs a doctor."

"Well, Josiah isn't exactly a doctor, but he's about the next best thing. He can take a look at Joe and tell us how to proceed from there. Are you okay hanging out with Brody for a bit?"

I nod but then realize he can't see me over the phone. So I reply, "Sure. I'll get us a bite to eat. Maybe that will distract Brody from what's going on with his dad."

"You can try, but I don't know how successful you'll be. From what Joe tells me, Brody is a pretty picky eater."

I glance over at Joe. His head is leaned up against the wall and he is snoring softly. "Well, I guess I'll just take my chances. Tell your security guy that Joe is in the pharmacy area near the blood pressure machine."

"Okay, will do. Josiah should be there shortly. Thanks for taking care of my friends."

"Um, how will I know who Josiah is?"

"He'll be wearing one of my crew jackets that says 'Security'. Even without it, though, it's hard to miss him. He gives new meaning to the words military bearing," Aidan responds.

"Okay, thanks. I'll keep an eye out for him. I need to go. Brody looks upset."

I hit the off button and slide the phone back into Joseph's pocket. When a store employee wanders by, I point to the basket in front of Brody's feet. "Can you do me a favor and check us out. I need to stay with my friend. He's not feeling well."

The store clerk's eyes widen. "Maybe we should call an ambulance."

"Oh, please don't. I have medical help coming and I don't want to upset his son with the commotion." I pull my credit card out of my pocket and hand it to her. "Please just check us out and let my friend have his privacy. He's already sick enough. He wouldn't want the whole world to know."

"Okay, but if help doesn't come soon, I need to tell my manager."

"I understand. But someone will attend to my friend

shortly."

The store clerk takes the basket and my credit card and heads toward the checkout stand.

I can feel Brody's hand tremble in mine and it breaks my heart.

I sit down on the floor beside Joseph and pat my lap. "You look like you could use a hug. I know I could. Do you want to sit here?"

Brody rocks up on the balls of his feet, in a gesture I've determined means he's stressed. Even so, he comes over and sits beside me on the floor. Very carefully, he places his head on my shoulder.

I place my arm around his shoulder. "I'm sorry your daddy is sick. You know, this happened to me once too. When I was a kid, I wasn't feeling so great, but the fair was in town. I wanted to go really bad. So, I fibbed to my family and told them I was fine. I wasn't really okay. So, right in the middle of the midway, I fainted. My cousin was throwing darts at the balloons, and the next thing he knew, I crumpled to the ground. I was feeling so awful, I didn't even want to move. My parents took me to the emergency room and they discovered that I had a severe case of tonsillitis. I had to take some medicine, but it didn't take me too long before I felt better. Hopefully, they'll figure out what's wrong with your daddy too. Maybe he just needs a little medicine and some rest."

Just then, a guy wearing all black strides up to me carrying a bag. When he sees Joseph, he shakes his head in dismay. "Joe, buddy, what did you do to yourself?" he asks as he pulls a stethoscope and ear thermometer out of his bag.

Joseph's eyes open just a fraction. "Hey, JoJo. Don't feel so good. Brody made a friend and she's so pretty," he mumbles.

Briefly, Josiah's eyes flick over to me before he returns to taking a set of vitals. "Leave it to you to pick up a beautiful woman when you're sick as a dog. Let's get you home and I'll call Aidan's concierge doctor. Heaven knows you don't need to run into the paparazzi looking like this. It would start never-ending rumors."

Josiah helps Joseph stand up. From what I can tell, Josiah is supporting most of his body weight.

"What now?" I ask.

"I think I'll have better luck getting him into the SUV. I can send someone to pick up his car later."

Brody stops in his tracks.

"Is there a problem?" I ask as I glance down at my new friend.

He shrugs off his backpack and pulls out a spiral notebook with the name of his preschool emblazoned across the front.

"Oh, you've got school tomorrow?" I guess.

Brody stares at me intently. He points at his notebook again. This time, he pulls out a piece of paper. I quickly scan it.

"I see. You've got a field trip to the zoo tomorrow. I wouldn't want to miss that either." I turn to Josiah. "You mind if I follow you home in Joseph's car? It seems Brody has a very important engagement tomorrow."

Josiah shrugs. "I don't see why not. The boss man says you have top security clearance. Besides, if we leave Joe's car here, it might attract some unwanted attention."

As we make it to Josiah's SUV, Josiah hands me a set of keys. I squeeze Brody's hand. "Okay, Brody. Let me buckle you in. I'll be right behind you in your dad's car."

Instead of getting in the SUV, Brody hugs my leg.

"Get out of town!" Josiah exclaims. "I've known Joe for a few years now and I've never seen Brody touch anyone else, let alone like that."

I shrug. "Umm, I guess Brody is riding with me. I just hope Joe's car is an automatic. It's been years since I've driven a car with a clutch. If it isn't, you and I could be in for a bumpy ride, Brody."

CHAPTER THREE

JOE

SOMETHING BUZZES NEAR MY ear. I slowly open my eyes. *Man! I feel like death warmed over.* I quickly close them when I start to feel dizzy. My throat is on fire. I haven't felt this bad since Kara-Jane gave me the finger and sent me on my way. I tried to drown my sorrows for months. I know I haven't done any drowning recently, so I don't know what happened.

When the noise in my ear becomes more insistent, it dawns on me that I'm in my room and that's my alarm clock. How did I get here? Last I knew, Brody was having a meltdown in the dairy aisle.

Brody! Where in the heck is Brody?

I try to get up and lose my balance. I knock a stack of books off my nightstand and let loose with a few curse words.

Brody comes running into my room with a toothbrush hanging out of his mouth. I blink to clear my vision. Instead of wearing his pajamas, he is dressed in his school uniform and his hair is neatly combed.

"Brody, who's here?" I ask suspiciously.

Brody makes a weird gesture with his hand and then runs out of my room.

As I struggle to pick up all the stuff I spilled on the floor, Brody comes back in my room, dragging someone behind him by the hand.

I fight to focus my eyes and I am floored when I come face-to-face with the enchanting goddess from the grocery store.

"Oh good, you're awake!" She walks over to my dresser. "The doctor says you need to take one of these every four hours until they're gone. Don't skip any doses. You're very sick. If you don't take your medicine, you could end up in the hospital. Josiah told me that if that happens, it would be a public relations nightmare for you guys and I believe him. I remember when Tasha and Jude got strep throat and the tabloids went nuts. If you end up in the hospital, it would only be worse."

"Doctor? When did I see a doctor? I only have a stupid cold. I decided I didn't really have time to go in."

"Well, let's put it this way ... your body and your bodyguard decided differently. Dr. Wright paid you a house call, compliments of your boss. You must've been too out of it to remember. He put you on some industrial-strength medicine to clear up your sinus infection. If this doesn't work, he's going to send you to a specialist."

I roll my eyes. "Oh great! Aidan and the band are going on tour in a few weeks and I have to learn all the backup vocals. Who stayed with Brody?"

She bites her lip. "Umm ... me. It was pretty late when the doctor finally left. I didn't know who was who in your contact list. I didn't want to make things awkward. Josiah didn't think you have any family around. Brody seems to like me okay, so I stayed.”

“So … you just volunteered to babysit a kid you met while he was having a meltdown in the middle of the dairy aisle? If you're after dirt on Aidan and Tara, I don't have any. I'm just the background singer. I play a little guitar and sing on a few songs, but I'm not really a target.”

She bristles. “I didn't get a chance to fully introduce myself to you before things got crazy last night. My name is Brynley Meeker. I've spent several years working for Locate My Heart. I'm about to start a practicum helping abused kids with the County. I'm getting my Master's degree in social work. I'm pretty good at sign language because special education was my minor until I decided not to be a teacher. By that time, I had almost enough credits to officially get a minor… Oh, listen to me, I'm babbling. Anyway, I wouldn't do anything to harm you or Brody. I don't kick my friends when they're down.”

I scrub my hand down my face. “You're right. I'm not being fair. You really stepped up for me. These days, it's easy for me to assume the worst after everything that's happened to Katelyn, Tasha, and Mindy. Do you know them?” I ask, as the random thought occurs to me.

Brynley smiles. “I wish. I'm just a fan. I met Aidan once at one of Kendall's benefits. I think I may have seen you at Kendall and Jameson's wedding. There were so many people there, I lost track of everyone.”

“How is it that you're tight with my friends and we've never met before yesterday?”

“Small world, but not small enough?” Brynley answers. “I need to get Brody to school. He has a field trip today.”

“How do you know that?”

“In his own way, Brody told me.”

"Do you even know where his preschool is?" I ask as I watch Brody give Brynley his coat.

She immediately helps him put it on and adjusts his backpack. "Did you put your lunch in your backpack?" she asks Brody.

My son reaches back and pats his backpack and grins.

"I think I know where his school is. The Internet is a powerful thing. I will be back to fix you breakfast after I drop him off."

"You don't have to do that," I protest.

"Yes, I do. Doctor's orders. Lucky for you, Brody bought a ton of soup yesterday."

◆•◆

I stumble out of bed and make my way to the bathroom. As I make my way past the mirror, the image startles me. I look more like a monster than an award-winning songwriter and up-and-coming folk musician. After I take care of my business, I take stock of the bathroom. As a single dad, I often don't have time to keep things as clean as I'd like, but somehow my living environment has suddenly been upgraded.

Cautiously, because my balance is a bit iffy, I make my way to the kitchen. I start to fill my coffee machine, but notice it's already been preloaded. I push the on button and suddenly feel a little woozy. So, I make my way to one of the chairs around the dining table.

I sit down and regain my bearings. That's when I notice that all the laundry that was stacking up in the utility room is now neatly folded and sitting on the arm of my couch. All the junk mail has been neatly stacked in the middle of the table and all the old chip wrappers and soda cans have been removed. It even looks like my floor has been mopped. Scout's muddy paw prints are nowhere to be found.

My coffee maker beeps and I attempt to get up and get some coffee. Unfortunately, another round of dizziness hits and I have to sit back down. When in the world did a simple cold evolve into this garbage?

I jump when I hear my front door open. I find the fact that Scout didn't even bark a little disconcerting. Before I can say anything Brynley comes in the kitchen with her hands on her hips. "Hey you! Can't you follow instructions? I told you to stay in bed and I would be back to fix you breakfast."

I didn't expect to be confronted in my own kitchen, so I snap back, "I don't recall appointing you as my keeper."

Brynley's face reddens. "Okay, that's fair. You didn't exactly appoint me. I volunteered. Heaven knows you need one. Dr. Wright said if you weren't famous, he would have stuck your butt in the hospital. I think you should pay attention to that."

I groan as I pull a paper towel off the roll and blow my nose. "I probably would if I could actually think. But I'm so dizzy I can't even form a coherent thought."

"Yeah, that's why I told you to stay in bed. Dr. Wright says your sinus infection has progressed to your middle ear. That's why you feel so lousy. You need to eat, drink some fluids, and take your medicine."

Brynley takes a shopping bag off her shoulder and places it on the kitchen counter.

"I didn't know what kind of appetite you would have this morning. So, I got a little bit of everything. What would you like for breakfast?"

"A nap?" I joke. "Seriously, you don't have to do all this for me, Brynley. I'm just some guy you met at the grocery store."

Brynley sets a hot cup of coffee in front of me and brings me the sugar bowl. "No, you're the friend of a friend and you're Brody's dad. Apparently, your son took a shine to me and I don't desert my friends."

"Still, this is a lot. You didn't have to get involved. You could've just called the ambulance, or something."

Brynley shrugs. "I could have, but the drama would have upset Brody. Besides, I take care of people. It's what I do. In fact, it's kind of who I am."

I sigh. "If that's true, you're one special kind of unicorn. Not many people around like you."

"If you say so," Brynley remarks as she rolls her eyes. "So, you never answered my question. What do you want for breakfast?"

I cringe as I swallow a sip of coffee. It feels like I swallowed shards of glass. "I don't know how much I can eat. My throat really hurts."

Brynley gives me a look of sympathy as she pulls the groceries out of the bag. "I'm sorry you're in pain. I tried to pick things that would be easy to eat. Look! I bought you Malt-o-Meal. I was even able to find it in chocolate for Brody."

Wrinkling my nose, I shake my head. "I couldn't stand that stuff as a kid, I don't think I could stomach it now."

Brynley looks a little deflated. "Oh … okay. That's okay. I have another plan. How do you feel about a nice fluffy, cheesy omelet? I can even put some bacon in it if you'd like."

At that moment, my stomach growls audibly. "Well,

I guess that's your answer. As much as I hate to say it, maybe we should skip the bacon for now — even though I'm starving."

"Okay, one very fluffy, cheesy omelet — without toast or bacon on the side — coming up. You need to go put on your most comfortable pajamas and find a movie to watch on TV. The doctor said you need to rest."

I sigh. "Okay, but does the doctor know we're going on tour soon? I have a ton of new songs to memorize before we go. I don't want to make an idiot of myself on stage."

Brynley walks over and squats down in front of me. "Look, I know you're frustrated. But if you don't take care of yourself now, you're not going to make it on the stage. You need to give yourself a break. Let me pamper you for a while."

"I'm not sure I even remember what the word means."

"Well, maybe it's time someone gave you a lesson in random acts of kindness. I specialize in those."

CHAPTER FOUR

BRYNLEY

AFTER JOE LEAVES THE kitchen, Scout scratches on the door to be let out. After a moment of indecision, I let him out into the backyard. I saw Brody do this a few times last night and this morning. Hopefully, I haven't made a huge mistake.

With one eye on the back window, I put the extra food away in the refrigerator and pantry. I hope Brody likes Malt-o Meal. He has two boxes now. I breathe an audible sigh of relief when I hear Scout scratching at the door to be let in. He comes in and stands in front of his bowl with a pathetic look on his face. "Okay, buddy. I have to find where they've hidden your food." With that, Scout scampers off to the laundry room and paws at a closed cupboard. When I open it, he starts whining. I pick up the small bag of dog food and read the back of the bag. Wow, he sure eats a lot less than the Newfoundland I dog-sat for the other day. I pour a small amount in his bowl. "I see Brody isn't the only one who has nonverbal communication down to a science. I got you fed, now I have to take care of your master."

Scout follows me into the kitchen after he takes a few bites of food.

With years of practice earned from taking care of my large family, I whip up a cheese omelet. As I'm waiting for the eggs to cook, I look around the townhouse. I miss taking care of people. I loved cooking for my family, but they haven't spoken to me in years. Turn down one arranged marriage when you're sixteen and no one wants to speak to you. Most of the time, I try to keep myself so busy I don't think about what I'm missing. But being dropped in the middle of this family where they clearly love each other is enough to bring all my pain rushing back. Not enough to marry Manfri, of course, but still…

I search around for a plate. A package of festive Christmas napkins falls on my head when I open an upper cupboard. Since the package is open, I help myself to one and put the rest back. I whimsically arrange his food on a plate and place it on a tray together with a glass of orange juice and the newspaper I found on the front stoop when I took Brody to school. Part of me wishes I had a vase and some flowers. But something tells me Joseph may not be as dedicated to fancy decor as I am.

I balance the tray like the waitress I once was and carry it upstairs.

When I enter Joseph's room, he is scowling at the TV and hitting buttons on his remote. Cautiously, I ask, "Is everything okay?"

He looks startled to see me and then just shakes his head in dismay. "Yeah, Brody keeps deleting my recordings on the DVR so he can record his favorite shows. I really wanted to see that game too."

I set the tray down on the nightstand. "Here, let me help you sit up so you can eat." I reach my hand out to help him sit up against the pillows.

"I shouldn't need help just to sit up in bed. This is ridiculous."

"So is the cost of gas. But it is what it is."

He flashes me a tight grin. "I suppose you're right, but I don't have to like it."

"I got news for you, Joe. Nobody likes being sick. It doesn't matter if you're eight months, eight years, or eighty years old. It still is a bummer." After I get him situated, I hand him the tray.

Joseph's eyes widen when he sees the gigantic omelet I made. "How many eggs did you use?"

I shrug. "You said you were starving. I took you at your word."

He nods and takes a bite. After he swallows, he says, "I'm glad you made me a bunch. It really hits the spo—"

Joseph stops mid-sentence when he sees the napkin I placed on the tray. "Where did you get this?" he demands.

"It actually hit me on the head. Isn't it festive? I thought it might make you smile."

"Not possible. I only kept these because Brody loved them, but they were in the back of the cupboard."

"Umm … about that," I reply, uneasily. "Your cupboards might be slightly rearranged. Brody and I were looking for his lunch pail, so I could pack his lunch today."

"Brody doesn't even eat cold lunch. His preschool provides a hot food lunch."

"Well, I didn't know that. I figured he'd need a sack lunch for his field trip. Besides, It's not like he could actually tell me. I hope he likes the peanut butter and banana sandwich I made for him. He smiled while I was making it. So, I hope that means good things."

Joseph sighs. "You're right. Here I am being a jerk when you're doing your best to cope with all this. It's just that these napkins have some baggage."

I sit down on a blanket chest next to the bed and put a throw pillow behind my back. "It's not like I'm going anywhere. You want to tell me how paper napkins can carry baggage?"

Joseph puts his fork down and runs his fingers through his long shaggy hair. "No, not really. But since I practically bit your head off, I probably owe you an explanation."

I shake my head. "Don't be silly. That's not the way random acts of kindness work. You don't owe me anything."

"Just because you're taking care of me doesn't mean I get to chew you out over nothing. Those napkins were the first thing Kara-Jane and I bought after I sold my first song. It was a great Christmas. Brody was old enough that he was delighted by everything."

"What happened to Kara-Jane?" I ask with trepidation. It would be just like me to fall for a random, drop-dead gorgeous stranger in the grocery store who is already married.

Joseph shrugs and starts to cough. When he stops, he says, "Beats me. Last I saw her, she was packing her things and playing kissy-face with Billy John Lovejoy. By the way, this was right after she wrecked my van with Brody inside. It was not a great week."

I grimace. "Should I even ask who Billy John is?"

"He is an ex-friend and bandmate. I knew he

thought he was hot stuff and God's gift to women. I just didn't think my wife would fall for his line of bull crap."

"Ouch! I take it you all are no longer working together?"

"Oh heck no! The rest of the guys voted him out. Billy John might've been a heck of a musician, but he violated a sacred rule of being in a band. You don't poach."

"That sucks. I'm sorry."

"Yeah, it stings for sure. I thought we were going to live happily ever after — especially after Brody was born. For an embarrassingly long amount of time, I waited for Kara-Jane to come back. She grew up in a very strict household. So, I figured she was just sowing her oats, so to speak. But, she never bothered to return to her husband and son. Last I heard, she and Billy John have twin daughters."

"But … but what about Brody?" I stammer. "I mean, I don't have any kids yet, I help Locate My Heart find them. Those parents are torn up. How do you just dump your kid, even if your relationship sucks?"

Joseph pauses to drink some orange juice. "Maybe I'm just an idiot, but I didn't think our relationship sucked so bad. I thought we were just experiencing growing pains after Brody was born. It was obvious Kara-Jane didn't like being stuck at home with Brody after he was born, but I figured she'd get used to our new routines. I'm sure Brody has questions, I have no idea what to tell him. I haven't figured out the answers for myself yet."

"Maybe this is one of those times where you just tell him you don't understand either. I'm sure it had nothing to do with Brody. He needs to know that."

Joseph rakes his hand through his hair. "I don't

know. Maybe I was a terrible husband and just didn't see it. I was busy finishing up my degree to become a special ed teacher and doing gigs with the band on the side to make money to pay the bills. If I would've paid more attention to her, maybe she wouldn't have strayed and Brody would still have a mom."

I lean forward. "Or maybe you could have done all those things and she still would have left. Sometimes couples grow apart instead of together."

Joseph's brows furrow. "I suppose, but it certainly wasn't the way I planned for things to go. I never in a million years thought I would be a single dad like my father."

"I don't know what happened to your mom, but obviously, your dad did a great job. You're a teacher, right? And your music is phenomenal. I love listening to you play the guitar."

"My mom didn't get a chance to leave. Ovarian cancer took her when I was about Brody's age. My dad says it's a shame because my mom was a great music teacher. She even played with the Boston orchestra once."

"I'm sorry for your loss. It's cool that you carried on her musical legacy, though. From what I can tell, you're an amazing father."

Joseph coughs violently for a few moments before he rolls his eyes at me. "Oh yeah, I'm such a great dad that my kid will be in kindergarten soon and still doesn't talk."

"Obviously, I don't know the whole situation with Brody. But, unless you're abusing him, I suspect his lack of verbal abilities has nothing to do with your parenting abilities. The fact that you stick around and treat your son with respect despite his disability shows that you are actually a spectacular dad."

"I'm not a loser. I won't ditch my kid because he can't talk. It's a parenting challenge I never anticipated, but Brody is a good kid," Joseph answers defensively.

I smile as I get up to take Joseph's empty plate away. "Exactly what I was saying. Maybe Brody is better off with one parent who loves him to pieces than two parents if one is indifferent. Anyway, I'm sorry I brought up old wounds. You're supposed to be focusing on getting better, not beating yourself up over the past."

Joseph laughs wryly. "Indifferent. That would pretty much sum up Kara-Jane. She's clearly indifferent toward Brody, our love story, and the life we hoped to build together."

"I'm sorry. You deserve better. I'm a firm believer in karma, though —"

Joe smiles wryly. "Karma has been treating me okay since the split. Aidan O'Brien hired me based on the breakup song I wrote after Kara-Jane left. Then, Tristan's friend, Jameson, needed someone to sublet his place when he fell in love with Kendall and moved to Oregon. He let me have it for dirt cheap, so I was able to save up enough money to move to Oregon too."

"Oh wow! I just assumed you were from here. You have the Pacific Northwest vibe down pat."

Joseph rubs his beard. "Yeah, definitely more comfortable to wear this here than in Florida. I kinda dig thermal shirts and flannel too."

"How did Brody take the move? Is he looking forward to starting school with the big kids in a couple of months?"

As he slumps against his pillow, Joseph sighs. "I wish I knew for sure. He seems okay, but it's hard to tell.

Although he seems to like his preschool, he doesn't have any friends yet. I take him to Madison and Trevor's for equine therapy. He is all smiles when we go there. I suspect he misses the sunshine, though. We used to play in the ocean all the time in Florida and it's too cold to do that here."

"If I were in his shoes, I would choose horses over cold water and sand every time. I think he got the better end of the deal."

"I hope so. After my dad died, I didn't really have much to keep me in Florida. I stayed a while, hoping Kara-Jane would come back. After a while, I decided I needed a fresh start. I just wish Brody could tell me how he really feels. Maybe, I would feel less guilty about pulling up all of his roots and moving him clear across the country."

I flinch. "My gosh! You haven't had an easy time of it. I'm sorry about your dad."

"I appreciate that, but my dad was so sick in the end that he was happy to go. I'm just focusing on the fact that he's no longer in pain."

"Well, I guess that's a silver lining. Can I ask you a personal question?"

He raises an eyebrow. "Were we making a distinction?"

I blush. "I guess not. I was wondering why Brody doesn't speak. Was he always this way?"

Joseph shakes his head. "When Brody was a baby, he was a chatterbox. Then, the words and sounds just disappeared."

"Heartbreaking. Do they know why?"

He shrugs. "Some specialists theorize that it's autism. Other doctors have suggested that maybe he just doesn't want to talk since his language skills disappeared after his mom left. Very cynical doctors have looked at me funny like I'm causing it. So, no one is sure."

"Maybe it's an occupational hazard given where I work, but abuse can cause real symptoms —" I venture carefully.

Joseph scrubs his hand down his face as he glares at me. "Look, I know I look rough and tough and it's not usual for dads to be single parents. But here I am. Unless you count limiting his video game time as abuse, I've never done anything to harm my child. If you think otherwise, you can just leave!"

I place my hands in front of me in a gesture of supplication. "Joseph, I don't think you hurt Brody. I'm just saying that I understand why the question was asked. In my field, if we don't ask when things are unusual, it's negligence. The doctors are in the same bind."

"On some level, I guess I get that. But it still burns my butt to think people might believe I'm causing Brody to be this way. I would give anything for him to be able to talk. I miss my little boy."

"I know I just met you guys yesterday, but Brody is pretty expressive even if he is silent. I don't think it's a matter of intelligence or anything. He played an important role in your rescue yesterday. It's clear he's very worried about you." I stand up to leave. "On that note, I should probably let you rest."

Joseph puts a hand up to stop me. "Not so fast! You know all of my deep, dark secrets. What about you? What's your story?"

His intense gaze stops me in my tracks. "I don't really have a story," I blurt.

Joseph coughs and shakes his head. "I don't believe

that. Everybody has a story. So, why are you here with me instead of at home with your husband and kids?"

I swallow hard. "Well, that's a long story. How much do you know about the Roma people?"

"Enough to know that calling them Gypsies is a racial slur. Kara-Jane used to watch this stupid reality show about over-the-top weddings."

I breathe out a sigh of relief. "Well, I guess you know more than most people. Anyway, I am a Romani. My parents are very old-fashioned and they wanted me to marry a son of a prominent member of our community. Manfri is a nice enough guy, but when I marry, I want to be in love with my husband."

Joseph's eyes widen. "You mean like an arranged marriage? I didn't think those still existed."

"I don't know if it's as formal as all that. But I was feeling lots of pressure. I always had dreams of becoming a teacher and getting married as a teenager wasn't in the cards for me."

"I don't blame you. If my dad had his way, I would have married the pastor's daughter. Of course, had I done that, I might still be married, but … whatever."

I wrinkle my nose. "Something tells me I'm a little too headstrong for a guy like Manfri. He wanted someone to stay home and cook his meals and have his babies." I shrug. "I had more ambitious plans."

"What did your family think of those plans?" Joseph asks with an expression of open curiosity.

"Apparently, they hated them because they stopped talking to me when I refused to get married."

"That's so many kinds of wrong I can't even wrap my brain around it. So you've been on your own since you were a teenager?"

I nod and try to blink back tears. No matter how long ago it's been, this is still a very painful subject for me. I never thought my whole family would turn their backs on me.

"Yeah, at first it seemed like a big adventure. After all, I was used to traveling around a lot with my family. My dad is a welder and we would go wherever there was a construction boom. I stayed at homeless shelters and youth hostels for a while until a foster family took me in. Mostly, I was just lonely."

Joseph smiles grimly. "I was impressed by your generous spirit before, but I'm even more awed now. Thank you so much for taking care of me and my son. Can I ask you one favor, though?"

I look at him quizzically. "Sure… I guess."

"Call me Joe. That's what all my friends call me and after all you've done, you are most definitely a friend."

I can't disguise my wide grin. "Oh good!" I hop on the bed beside him and grab for the remote.

He holds the remote away and laughs. "Hey! What are you doing? You may not want to get too close. I'm pretty sick. I don't want you to get sick too."

"Too late, friend, I've already been exposed to all your cooties." I grab the remote and point it at the TV. "Since I'm your friend that means I get to choose what we watch, right?"

Joe groans. "I don't think that's the way it works. Doesn't the sickest person get to choose?"

I ponder that idea for a minute. "Okay, I get to choose, but you have veto power. Then, you choose the next thing, fair?"

Sinking further down into the pillows, Joe says, "I'm not sure I have enough energy to care. Just try not to choose something totally obnoxious."

"How about something nostalgic?"

"Please don't subject me to endless *Golden Girls* reruns," Joe pleads with a chuckle as he closes his eyes.

"That wasn't my plan, but if I ever need to torture you, now I know how to do it."

I click the remote and the TV changes. Joe opens his eyes and glances over at me with surprise. "I've got a satellite system with like a billion channels and you choose *The Price is Right?*"

"What can I say? When I was sick as a little kid, I had to go over to my grandma's house and she watched this show religiously. So we would snuggle and grandma would feed me ginger ale and chicken soup. I always felt better after staying at my grandma's house. You never know, this show could be the secret ingredient that makes you feel better."

Joe nods. "You may be on to something there. I remember watching the *Price is Right* when I was little too. It didn't make my mom better, but she had cancer. Maybe its restorative value is only if you have the cold or flu."

"So, what do you say? Are you going to exercise your veto?"

Joe shakes his head, "Nah, I'm not going to argue with grandmas everywhere. Let's hope the contestants win a lot of stuff."

I hand Joe his unfinished orange juice. "Drink, it's good for you."

He makes a sour face. "I'd rather have coffee — or is that off-limits for my recovery?"

Mary Crawford

I set the remote down and jump off the bed. "No, I just forgot to put it on the tray. Be right back and then the healing marathon can begin."

Chapter Five

Joe

As I wait for come back upstairs, my phone rings. I reflexively answer it. It's probably Josiah checking in on me.

"Go for Joe," I instruct.

"Is this Mr. Summers?" a voice at the other end asks.

"It is. Who is this?"

"Oh, hi Mr. Summers. This is Felicity Appleton, I'm a preschool teacher in Brody's class at ABC Learning Academy."

"Is Brody hurt?" I ask with alarm.

"No, nothing like that. I just thought you might be interested in hearing about Brody's language breakthrough."

"He talked to you?"

"No, not in so many words. But it was close. A group of boys cornered him in the reading corner. Before I could get back there to stop them, Brody was calling them big chickens."

Brynley comes back in my bedroom and I motion for her to be quiet as I process what I was just told.

"You're telling me that my son, who doesn't talk, was calling other students names?"

"That's my understanding, yes. Chickens, to be exact."

"Chickens?" I repeat blankly. "Brody doesn't speak, how is that possible?"

Brynley sets the coffee down on my nightstand and sits on the edge of my bed. "Umm … that might be my doing. I don't know if you remember this, but last night I taught Brody how to sign the word chicken when we were buying soup."

I raise an eyebrow at Brynley before I ask "Mrs. Appleton, are you telling me Brody was calling people names in sign language and it was serious enough to warrant a call home?"

"Well…uh…yes. It is the first time Brody has been documented using any kind of language, as far as I know."

"So, Brody isn't in any trouble?"

"No, sir. I just wanted to let you know your son is using language skills — even if it is in a rather inappropriate manner."

"Oh, okay. Thanks for letting me know. I'll have a discussion with him about calling other people names, though."

"No problem, Mr. Summers. With any luck, this will be the thing that breaks open the language dam. I have to get back to the students. But I thought you might want to know."

"Thank you for sharing. Have a good day." I hang up the phone.

I turn to Brynley with an amused expression. "Of all the words you could've taught him, you chose chicken?"

She blushes. "Okay, in my defense, in context, it made perfect sense."

"Crap! I knew I shouldn't have listened to that specialist. But, he seemed to know what he was talking about —"

"What specialist? Sorry, I don't know your whole back story, so I'm a little lost."

"I've taken Brody to dozens of doctors trying to figure out how to help him. One of the specialists instructed me not to teach him any sign language because if he wasn't required to rely on his voice, he would never talk again. I should know better. I work with a trained sign language interpreter and a deaf musician. I don't know why I chose to follow his advice."

"I know it's hard when you get contradictory advice. My grandma had stomach issues and every doctor she went to told her to do something different to manage it."

"I should've just followed my gut. I was just afraid to do something wrong. Maybe I should teach him a bunch of signs. He could hang out with Aidan and Tara and I bet he would pick up stuff really easily. He's super smart."

"If he is taunting bullies with a word he just learned last night, I'd say so. I can work with him if you want. Like I said, I minored in special education. I've taken a bunch of ASL classes. I'm not as good as Tara, but I know the basics."

A tear leaks out of the corner of my eye as I consider the ramifications. "What if he's been searching for a way to communicate for years and I withheld it?"

Brynley grabs my hands and squeezes them. "You were just trying to follow medical advice. It sounds like maybe Brody needs a different approach, but that doesn't mean you did anything wrong. I know from personal experience that you can't go back and undo the past, you can just learn from your mistakes and go forward."

"Just out of curiosity, what else did you teach my son while I was sleeping?"

"Well, I might have taught him the joy of a peanut butter and marshmallow fluff sandwich and my name sign," Brynley replies in an embarrassed tone.

I rolled my eyes. "Oh great! Brody can barely even talk to you and he's already conning you into loading him up with sugar. Just out of curiosity, is your name sign like a salute?"

Brynley bites her lip. "I suppose it looks a little like that. It's a B at temple level. Then you make the B sign mimic the waves in my hair."

I wish I felt like jumping up and down with joy. My eyes are lit up with glee as I explain, "You know what this means, right?"

Brynley shakes her head. "No, I guess I don't."

"You taught Brody two words last night. That's more progress than I've had with him in years of speech therapy."

Brittany grins from ear to ear. "Oh, that's great news!"

Even as the words of praise leave my mouth, I can't help but feel a knot of anxiety in the pit of my stomach. So, what's so special about Brynley? Why haven't I had that same kind of success?

I wake up to the sound of Scout's nails clicking on the wood floor. I hear Brynley say, "Okay! I think Brody gets the message you're happy to see him. Give him a second to get his coat and backpack off before you attack him for cuddles." She laughs out loud, but more astonishingly, so does Brody.

I draw in a quick surprised breath and it makes me cough. My ribs hurt and I have to hold them in an attempt to lessen the pain.

Brody runs around the corner. He is frowning mightily.

As soon as I catch my breath, I assure him, "I'm fine. I just have an icky upper respiratory infection. But the doctor has me on medicine. Until it kicks in, I will keep coughing."

Tentatively, Brody walks up to me and starts to study me. I take his hand and put it on my forehead. "See, I'm already feeling better. I'm not nearly as hot as I was this morning. Brynley is taking really good care of me."

Brody looks back and forth between us and smiles.

I struggle to sit up in bed and brace my back on the headboard. After I do, Brody hands me a can of ginger ale.

"Thanks, Buddy. I understand you used a new word at school today."

Brody's gaze drops to the floor and he squirms uncomfortably. He starts to bounce on the balls of his feet.

"It's okay, Brod. I'm not upset, although you probably shouldn't call your classmates farm animals. I just wondered if you want to learn some more words in the sign language."

He points to Brynley and uses her name sign.

I nod. "Yeah, Brynley said she would help teach you. She's probably a much better sign language teacher than me. She's taken classes and everything. I only know what Aidan and Tara taught me."

Brody stares at me. It's impossible to read his expression.

Undaunted, Brynley squats down in front of him and starts to sign as she voices. "Are you hungry? Would you like a snack? I bought some apples for your lunch. You can have one if you want. You can also choose your chocolate yogurt."

Brody looks back and forth between us and then makes a funny gesture in front of his nose.

"Chicken soup?" Brynley guesses. "I suppose that makes a good snack too. Your dad needs to eat too since he has to take some medicine." She turns to me. "Is chicken soup okay with you, or would you rather have something else?" she signs as she speaks.

I sign the words, "Okay… Thank you."

Brody grins and takes Brynley's hand as he escorts her out of my bedroom.

After a few minutes, the basketball game I'm watching becomes monotonous and I drift off to sleep. I wake up when there is a soft knock on my door. When I look up, Brody is carrying a plate full of sliced apples and crackers. Brynley is following him. "Brody wanted to carry the whole tray, so we negotiated a compromise," she explains.

Brody sets the plate on my nightstand with what can only be described as a flourish.

Brynley picks up the plate and puts it on the tray.

"You want to tell your dad what's on the menu for his afternoon snack?"

I hold my breath. Open-ended questions like that usually don't work very well with Brody. Brody glances up at Brynley.

She smiles down at him. "Go ahead. If you forget, I'll remind you."

Shyly, Brody turns to me and makes a motion against his cheek.

Brynley cheers, "Great job remembering!" She turns to me. "Brody says we are having apples for our snack."

Brody pulls on her shirttail. Then, he takes his fist and hits his other elbow.

Brynley's eyes light up. "You're right! We are having crackers. What else are we having?"

Brody looked lost for a second and then makes the funny sign in front of his nose.

"That's right. But don't forget the rest of the sign. The chicken has to peck or scratch the ground. Do you remember the sign for soup?" Brynley cups her hand in front of her chest.

Brody smiles and mimics her as he pretends to scoop up soup with two fingers from his other hand.

Brynley turns to me. "In case you missed our little sign language lesson, Brody just told you we are having apples, crackers and chicken soup for our snack. He has natural talent as a signer."

My eyes tear up and I turn my head to hide my emotions. Swallowing hard, I pivot back toward Brody. "You did great, Brody. Thank you so much for helping Brynley make me a snack." Remembering my manners, I sign, "Thank you."

"There is another word! Your dad just said thank you. You want to go eat using a TV tray while you watch your TV?" Brynley offers.

Brody nods ever so slightly.

"Okay, after we all eat dinner, I'll help you make a blanket fort. Do you have homework first?" Brynley asks with her hands on her hips.

Brody grins as he points to the sticker on his shirt, which says junior zookeeper.

"Oh, I forgot. You had a field trip today. Lucky you! Blanket forts it is."

"Brody is a little young for homework. I don't think they assign much in preschool."

Brynley shrugs. "I know. But if he gets used to thinking about it before he starts playing, it'll be easier later on."

"Smart! You don't have kids, how did you figure that out?"

Brynley swallows hard. "Lots of practice on my siblings and nieces and nephews. I guess I just picked things up along the way. My grandma never got to go to school. Back then, it wasn't really an option in our culture. So, she always made sure all the kids understood what a privilege it is to learn."

"I understand. My mother was a teacher before she died. So, I feel privileged to follow in her footsteps."

"Let's go downstairs and get your dinner tray. I bet you want to watch a dinosaur movie."

Brody nods enthusiastically.

I reach out and try to hug Brody. He flinches away and stands stock-still. I attempt to disguise my sigh as it becomes clear that adding a few words in sign language won't fix everything.

"Let me get Brody set, then I'll come back to check on you," Brynley says as Brody pulls her out of my room by her shirttail.

CHAPTER SIX

BRYNLEY

BRODY LOOKS WORRIED AS Brody looks worried as he glances back up the stairs. I grasp his hand and walk him toward what seems to be his favorite chair in the living room and put the movie on for him. I squat down in front of him and ask, using sign language and my voice, "Would you like chocolate milk or orange juice?"

He grins at the sign for chocolate milk and then laughs out loud when I sign orange juice. I have to admit, the sign for orange juice is a little funny. When he stops laughing, I sign again, "Chocolate milk, orange juice, which?

Slowly, he starts to move the C around in a circle on his other hand.

"Chocolate milk it is! You mind if I go up and check on your dad? He's having a rough day. If you need anything, just come up and get me."

I bring him his TV tray with his chicken soup, apples, crackers and chocolate milk. After I set it in front of him, he points to me and then points upstairs. He leans around me to watch the television.

I smirk at Brody's actions. He reminds me so much of my youngest brother. "Okay, message received. I can see I'm no longer needed here. I won't bug you while you're watching your movie. I'll just go keep your dad company."

Brody just waves me away.

Shrugging, I back into the kitchen and grab myself a bowl of soup and carefully climb the stairs to Joe's room.

When I enter Joe's room, I'm shocked to see that he's not eating. Instead, he's lying on his side. When he turns his head to look over his shoulder, his jaw is set and he glares at me.

"What's wrong with you? I was just gone for a few minutes." I brush my fingers over his shoulder. He jumps and rolls over before he searches the room for Brody.

"If you're looking for Brody, he's not here. He's downstairs watching his favorite *Land Before Time* movie. He wanted me to get out of his hair and come up to check on you. I guess it's a good thing he did. What happened? You were fine when I left."

Joe pulls himself up in bed and sits against the headboard. "No, I wasn't fine. Must be nice to be the only one to connect with Brody. Hey, I'm only his dad, but knock yourself out."

I recoil from his bitter words. "Umm … okay, I never meant to intrude. Give me a couple minutes to say goodbye to Brody and I'll be out of your hair," I reply in a shaky voice as I turn to leave the room.

Joe reaches out and snags the hem of my shirt. "I didn't mean it like that. Don't leave yet."

I turn around and cross my arms, almost hugging my body. "Seems pretty clear to me."

Joe shakes his head and starts to cough. Eventually, he sighs. "I'm sorry. Please stay and let me explain."

Unsure of what to do, I perch on the very edge of the bed as my thoughts tumble around.

"Listen, I don't mean to sound resentful. You've been wonderful."

"But?" I prompt.

"This is going to make me sound like a shallow jerk. But it is what it is. I've been taking Brody to therapists and specialists clear across this country trying to help him. Trying to connect in any way I can. Do you know he barely tolerates me if I try to comb his hair? It doesn't matter how gentle I am, he hates it with a passion. In fact, he doesn't even like me to touch him at all."

"I know, that's really hard."

"But it's not hard for you. That's the point. You met my son when he was at his most vulnerable — in the middle of a meltdown. Yet, he didn't shy away from you, he reached out – something I haven't seen him do since he was a baby. I'll tell you, that stings more than just a little bit. Not only that, you accidentally find a way to reach him and help him communicate. I don't even know how you did that. I've been trying to help my son communicate for years and you've already taught him more words in a few minutes than I have in years — despite all the therapy and specialists. I don't even know how to cope with that."

I reach out to brush a piece of lint off of the bed. "I don't know what to say, Joe. I guess sometimes fate puts us exactly where we're needed. I'm glad Brody connected with me. He's such a cool kid."

"He *is* a cool kid. That's why I'm pissed off that you're able to connect with him on a level I can't even begin to reach."

"Honestly, I don't know whether to be insulted or high-five you for having the guts to be honest. So, I'm just gonna give you the benefit of the doubt and give you kudos for letting me know how you feel."

"I don't know if I deserve a high five. I pretty much feel like pond scum. I can't believe I'm jealous of your relationship with Brody. You just met us yesterday."

"That may be true. But haven't you ever met someone you click so well with that you feel like you've known them your whole life?"

Joe nods. "Yeah, I feel that way with Declan. He would be my brother if I actually had one. We've been friends since the first second we met."

"Who's to say that didn't happen with Brody and me? Since he can't really tell us — yet, we'll have to guess."

"So you think this mystical connection you guys have is going to 'fix' him?"

"No! I never said that. I'm not a doctor, I am a newly minted social worker with a minor in special education. I went to pick up some chicken strips and JoJos from the grocery store and somehow got entangled in your life. If you don't want me here, I'll leave. You were so sick, I was just trying to help."

Joe growls in frustration. "I know! You didn't do anything wrong. It's just hard for me to accept that after all we've been through, Brody reached out to you instead of me. I shouldn't need that kind of help. What does that say about me as a parent?"

"It says you're in a tough situation made even harder by your illness. In case you haven't noticed, parents of completely typical children get tired, worn out, and sick too. It's not a character flaw."

"Yeah, I get that. But right now, I feel like the world's worst parent. I'm not sure if I'm ready to change everything in Brody's life just because he met a stranger in the grocery store. I don't know whether the specialist's approach is the right one, but — " he trails off and shrugs.

My heart breaks a little for Joe as he angrily swipes away tears. "I feel like all I ever say to you is 'I'm sorry'. I wish I had some answers for you, but I don't. So, if it's too disruptive for me to be in your life, I'll leave."

The silence stretches between us like a dark thundercloud. Finally, I hear Joe whisper, "Maybe that's what I am most afraid of. A big part of me doesn't want you to go. It's been a long time since I've connected with anyone like I have with you. But, I have to put Brody first. It might be best for you to leave before Brody gets too attached."

Joe's words feel like a sucker punch. Somewhere between the dairy food aisle and eating soup and crackers for dinner, these guys have worked their way deep in my heart.

My eyes burn with unshed tears as I whisper, "If that's the way you want it, I guess I'll leave after I put Brody to bed and tell him goodbye." I have to draw in a deep breath before I can continue. "I'll leave my contact information on the table. If you ever decide you're ready to open your heart and your mind to new options, you know where I am."

CHAPTER SEVEN

JOE

FOUR DAYS. THESE BEEN the longest four days of my life! I stare up at the ceiling as I cuddle an overtired, distraught Brody in the crook of my arm. It took him an hour to calm down and stop crying tonight. It's been this way every night since I told Brynley to go.

Brody is always a pretty somber little guy. He may smile at his cartoons, but he rarely smiles or shows any kind of emotion towards people. However, since I essentially kicked his favorite person out of the house, he has been almost inconsolable. He signs Brynley's name sign over and over and points at the door.

I'm such an idiot.

I asked her to leave because I didn't want her to disrupt our precious routine. I didn't want to feel like an ineffective parent. Her success with Brody hurt my ego. Instead of dealing with it like the grown man I'm supposed to be, I gave her the boot and blamed my decision on my son. Some hero I am! My dad would be so disappointed in me.

My dad also had a saying, "If you make a mistake,

don't keep making it just because you've gone down that path before."

It's time for me to see if I can rectify the biggest mistake I've ever made. It would serve me right if Brynley decided to wash her hands of us and move on with her life.

I unfold the piece of paper I've been carrying around in my pocket for three days. I know I need to make this call, but how exactly do you apologize for criticizing someone for being who they are and trying to help your son?

Blowing out a deep breath, I dial the number.

When Brynley picks up the phone, she sounds exhausted. "Brynley, this is Joe," I announce awkwardly.

"Hi, Joe. How are you feeling? Are you still taking your medicine?"

"I am. Dr. Wright ordered a chest x-ray. My respiratory infection is not clearing up as quickly as he would like it to, so he changed my antibiotics."

"Oh, I'm so sorry. I was hoping you would feel much better by now," Brynley says. Something is off. She doesn't sound like her usual self.

"Are you okay? I didn't make you sick, did I?"

"No, I'm fine. Actually, I'm not fine, but it's not because I caught your bug. It's just been a rough day at work."

"Can you tell me what happened?"

Brynley sighs. "I suppose. It's already all over the news websites. It was a horrifying day. You know what we do here at Locate My Heart, right?"

"I do. You help find missing kids. Your agency helped find my friend's baby brother. We travel in the same circles. I heard all about how Locate My Heart helped make Jameson's family whole again."

"Yeah, Toby's story had a super positive outcome. But unfortunately, they're not always happy. I guess I should be used to that by now, but this one hit me right in the heart."

"I wish I was there to," I clear my throat, "give you a hug."

"I need one. I can't help but feel like if I had done my job a little more efficiently or faster or contacted more people, this one would've turned out differently."

"What do you mean?" I ask, dismayed by the pain and recrimination in Brynley's voice.

"So, this guy who was completely strung out on drugs violated his restraining order and took two of his kids. By the time we could locate them, he killed the youngest one in front of his six-year-old brother."

I curse under my breath. "That's rough. I'm so sorry. You know it's not your fault, right? Clearly, he was deranged. No sane parent would ever do anything like that. So, it probably didn't matter when the kids were found. He would've likely done the same thing if you had located the kids sooner."

"In my heart, I know that. But every time I replay the scenario in my head, all I can see is that poor little boy watching his dad nearly decapitate his two-year-old brother. That kid is never going to be normal again."

"How is the mother handling this?"

"The word from Tyler is that she is in shock. I don't know much more — and that's probably a good thing. I don't even want to think about the ramifications for my job. If people stop trusting Locate My Heart to help find their missing children, it would be disastrous. In most situations, what we do is really helpful. It just hurts when we can't get there in time."

"I'm sorry I bothered you on such a tough day," I blurt.

"No, that's not what I meant. I'm so glad to hear your voice. I'm tired of listening to the thoughts in my head. Did you need something?"

"Yeah, I need to apologize for being a jealous, selfish jerk and minimizing the role you filled in my son's life. I am so sorry I disrespected you that way."

"That's nice to hear, but I need to know more. Is my role only in Brody's life?" Brynley presses.

"No. That's been the hardest realization for me. Obviously, I can't handle everything on my own. Even though I'm sick as a dog, the few days you were here were some of the best I've ever had. Brynley, my son isn't the only one who misses you. I think of you every single day. I'm sorry I screwed things up between us."

"I'm sorry too," her voice chokes up. "It seems like everyone I care about in my life tosses me away like I'm yesterday's garbage. I'm starting to wonder if it's just something about me."

"Brynley, there's absolutely nothing wrong with you. I was a moron. Is there anything I can say to convince you I want you in my life" I ask as I hold my breath.

"You've done a good job of apologizing. Even so, how do I know you won't change your mind again if I hurt your feelings? It's been a rough couple of days. I don't know if I could handle another disappointment. I am emotionally exhausted."

"If you come back, Brody and I have an endless supply of hugs. Let us take care of you for a change."

"It's a tempting offer, but I need to think about it

for a while. I don't want to set myself — or anyone else — up to get hurt."

"Brody has already been hurt," I protest.

"That's probably true, but that's not my fault. I just want to make sure I don't make a bad situation even worse. I'm not ready to risk a move, but I'll come visit with Brody and take him out to ice cream or something, so he doesn't feel abandoned."

My stomach drops to my feet. I guess I knew this could happen — but I was hoping my powers of persuasion would be a little more successful. I have to take a moment to regroup.

After a long pause, Brynley asks, "Are you still there, or did you hang up on me?"

"I'm still here, I'm just processing what you said."

"That's what I'm saying. I think we both need some time to process whatever this is between us and I don't want Brody to get caught in the middle."

"I don't like hearing that you don't feel comfortable coming back, but I understand."

Brynley sighs. "I'm sorry it has to be this way. I'm stuck in an impossible situation."

"I apologize for making everything awkward. I hope we can get back to the way things were."

"I hope so too. Still, the words you said cannot be unsaid. So, I don't know where that leaves us."

"I guess I'll have to convince you Brody and I deserve a second chance."

CHAPTER EIGHT

BRYNLEY

WEARILY, I SQUINT AT my computer screen and double-check it against the spreadsheet covering most of my desk. I pause to take another sip of coffee. I think this is my third cup of the day. At the rate I'm going, I'm going to get an ulcer.

Kendall walks by my desk with a stack of financial files in her arms. "Remind me why I love working here again?" I whine.

"Lucky for us, it's not always grant-writing season. If it was, I think I would lose my sanity. All the publicity we received over the last few years has been really good for awareness and donations, but it certainly complicates these grant applications."

"I wonder if Riker's death will discourage people from using our services?" I blurt the question which has been weighing heavily on my mind for the last week.

"That was a tough loss and I cried for a couple of days solid. Then, Jameson reminded me that we were able to find Carter alive. If we hadn't been involved, maybe it would've been too late for him too. Knowing that doesn't take the pain away, but it does allow me to sleep at night. My husband is right. We gave that case everything we had. Sometimes, everything just isn't enough and we can't save them all."

"Intellectually, I understand that. But when I lay down to go to sleep at night, I have horrific thoughts of what Carter must have witnessed. It's going to take me a long time to work through it."

Kendall walks over to give me a hug. "I'm sorry, Bryn. I wish we could save every single child. I won't tell you to grow a tougher skin. You're too much like me, and I know you put your whole heart into each and every case. Even though it's what makes you great at your job, every once in a while it's going to get broken."

"I suck at heartbreak, but it seems to be everywhere in my life."

The chime above the door sounds. Kendall looks over her shoulder. "That's probably Jameson. He said he was going to bring us something from Joy and Tiers for lunch. He is so sweet. He knows I get so anxious when I am working on grants that I forget to eat."

"Sorry to disappoint you gals, but I'm not bringing food," Denny says as he places a big bouquet of roses on the counter. "I'm glad your husband takes such good care of you, though."

"I wonder if these are for you or me?" I walk over and peek at the little note card sticking out of the bouquet. It has my name on it. I can't help but grin. I love flowers, especially roses.

"I do believe they are for you, Miss Brynley," Denny answers with a wink. "Your fellow must've done something to get himself in the doghouse."

I swing my gaze around and look at him in surprise.

"Well, kinda. But how did you know?"

"You see those yellow roses there? They say he's sorry. The white and red ones in the middle? Those are his way of saying he wants to be with you. It doesn't take a rocket scientist to figure out the two of you are having a rough patch. Your young man went to lots of trouble to send his apology. Maybe you should think about forgiving him. Good relationships are worth fighting for."

I cringe. "I'm not sure there actually is enough of a relationship between us to fight for."

Denny points to the large vase of flowers. "Are you sure? This is a pretty big statement."

I sigh as I bury my nose in the roses and inhale deeply. "These are so beautiful. I appreciate the gesture, I just don't know if it's enough to build a relationship on."

Denny nods. "I understand. These things take time, but don't forget your young man tried to make his wrong into right. I'm not trying to tell you how to run your life, but if you let misunderstandings fester, they sometimes can infect your whole relationship. You might want to try talking to your fella. After all, he made a grand gesture."

I reach out and touch one of the soft petals. "You're right, Denny. It was a lovely gesture. He should get credit for making it — even if I'm still angry with him."

"Okay, good luck with that. I have more deliveries to make and I don't want the flowers to wilt in my truck. You gals have a nice day."

Kendall waits impatiently as Denny leaves and gets in the big delivery van. I brace myself for the questions.

As soon as he leaves, Kendall whips out her cell phone and starts taking pictures of the bouquet. "So, are you going to tell me who these are from and why you don't look thrilled to get them. I know if I received these from Jameson, I would be over the moon."

I groan in frustration. "It's complicated."

Kendall stares at me thoughtfully. "Oh … Complicated like I need to call your cousin, the videographer, to film an upcoming wedding?"

I let out a surprised burst of laughter. "No! Well, not yet. Ack! This is so crazy! I can totally see myself walking down the aisle with this guy. That's a very dangerous thought."

Kendall practically drops her cell phone. "I was teasing! When in the world did you start dating? I haven't seen you with anyone since it didn't work out with my brother."

I hide my face behind my hair. "It was so cliché. I picked up a guy in the grocery store —"

"Is that a question or statement?" Kendall teases.

"A little of both, I guess. I still can't believe I met such a gorgeous guy when I stopped to help his son. To make matters worse, he's famous. Like I said, it couldn't get any more complicated."

"Famous people aren't any different from the rest of us. Look at our friends, Mindy, Tasha, Jude and Aidan are completely normal. Tristan isn't like a normal person, but he tries to be."

"You know Aidan pretty well?" I venture carefully. "What about the rest of the band?"

"Honestly, I know Mindy better than the rest of them because she used to come into the stationery and art store I worked at before I became director at Locate My Heart. She's all kinds of cool. Aidan has helped us out on several fundraisers. He and Tara are so generous. A while back, Jameson and I played pool with their bass player, Jerome. I had a good time, but Jamison wasn't having so much fun since he lost every round to Jerome. But they're all awesome."

"What do you know about their acoustic guitar player?"

Kendall smiles. "Oh my, he is a handsome one. He's pretty shy and doesn't hang out with the rest of the group much because he has a little boy with special needs. But I'll tell you, even though I am a happily married woman, I swoon a little when he sings. He's got that gravelly sexy voice — "

I nod without saying anything.

Kendall's jaw goes slack for a moment before she replies with wide eyes. "Wait a minute … Joe Summers has a little boy and you said you met someone who was devastatingly handsome with a little boy in the grocery store. Are you dating Joe Summers?"

I rubbed my temples. "I am — or, at least I was. Well, not exactly, but sort of, I guess. Now I don't know for sure what we're doing. The other day, he abruptly asked me to leave. Like I said, it's all impossibly complicated."

"I don't know exactly what's going on between the two of you, but it seems to me maybe Joe is regretting his decision to let you go. What are you going to do? These are beautiful flowers."

I shrug. "I suppose I'm going to call Joe to thank him for the flowers."

Kendall raises an eyebrow. "What else are you going to say?"

"I don't have a freakin' clue. Fortunately, Joe is going to the hospital to have a follow-up chest x-ray. So, I have a little bit of time to think about it."

"Don't think too hard," Kendall cautions.

"Sometimes overthinking is as harmful as impulsively following your heart."

I slip my feet into the big fuzzy slippers Brody picked out for me the last time we went to the mall and flop down into my favorite Papasan chair. There are a few things I miss about my apartment, this is one of them. I clutch my cell phone for a few seconds trying to gather the courage up to call. My heart wants to ignore all my doubts and forget about what happened. Unfortunately, I also have to deal with my head which tells me I don't have enough answers to make a decision yet.

I take a deep breath and dial Joe's number. He picks up on the first ring. "How is my favorite grown-up doing today?"

I groan. "I went into social work to help people. But lately, all I seem to be doing is paperwork. I know grants are important to the health of Locate My Heart, but I hate compiling all the data and trying to shape it into something that makes sense to someone who doesn't actually know the inner workings of what we do. We do so many things, it's hard to simplify it for the grant application process."

"I'm sorry, that must be frustrating."

I yawn and stretch out my arms. I'm getting cramps from typing so much. "If I ever win the lottery, I'm going to give Locate My Heart an operating budget for like ten years, so no one has to jump through these hoops."

Joe chuckles. "Yeah, it'd be nice to have that kind of money to give away. Umm … If everything went like it was supposed to go, you should have received something to brighten your day."

I blush, even though Joe can't see me over the phone. "Oh, I did! That's why I called. I wanted to thank you for the beautiful flowers, but then I got distracted when you asked me how my day went."

"I'm glad you like them."

"Oh, I love them! I've never received a big bouquet like that. Roses are my favorite flowers."

"Does that mean I'm forgiven?" Joe asks hopefully. "We miss you around here."

"Joe, we have issues to settle between us, which aren't going to be fixed with just flowers. Although they're beautiful, they don't answer my questions."

"Okay, I must be really slow. I was rude, and I apologized — repeatedly. What am I missing?"

I pause for a moment to organize my thoughts. It's hard to articulate what I don't fully understand myself. "Okay, this may sound weird and disjointed, but try to be patient with me. I thought everything was going really well and I was doing a pretty good job of helping you both. I love making you guys happy. Then, suddenly, you weren't happy. In fact, you were livid. I don't know exactly what I did to tick you off. If I don't understand that, I'm not sure there's any point in me coming back."

Joe blows out a breath of frustration. "I thought I was coping just fine with Brody's limitations. I tried really hard to do all the speech therapy and make sure Brody is healthy. Nothing I did seemed to help. Then, you literally bump into us and everything changed. Instead of shying away from you, Brody treated you like you were his long-lost friend. Not only that, he started using words with you. Maybe they're sign language words, but it's still communication. That's a luxury I've never had with him."

"So, you're mad that Brody made a friend?" I press.

"It's complicated. On the one hand, I am really grateful. On the other hand, I hate that my son isn't friends with me."

"Maybe Brody gravitated toward me because he felt like I could understand him. I think if you learn Brody's language, you'll get that he considers you his best friend."

"You really think so?" Joe asks softly.

"I do. Maybe you should work on learning to speak his language so you can find out for yourself."

"I've got nothing else to lose. The approach the specialist suggested obviously isn't working."

"Sometimes, change can be just the thing you need to move forward."

"Thanks for calling, Brynley. I'll touch base with you later."

As I hang up the phone, I wonder if my insistence on answers is more harmful than helpful. Every time I talk to him, I'm tempted to run into Joe's arms and never leave. But even as I have that thought, I know we have serious issues to work out before we move forward — that is, if I haven't blown my chance.

⎯⎯⎯⎯⟩●⟨⎯⎯⎯⎯

"Good morning, Brynley. Would you like your usual?" Heather asks me as I finally reach the front of the line at Joy and Tiers.

"Mmm-hmm. It's been an insanely long couple of weeks. I need dark roast stat!"

"If you can wait around for about six minutes, I've got pecan sticky buns coming out of the oven."

My stomach growls audibly. "Sounds good to me!"

I walk over to the lounge area in the bakery and sit

down. My phone buzzes to indicate I have an email. *I wonder what obscure number Kendall needs now?* Reluctantly, I check my email messages. I'd rather not have to dig up any more data today. I have a raging headache and my eyes hurt from looking at the screen so much.

When I open my email application, I notice the email is from Joe. I have no idea why he's sending me emails. Curious, I pull the iPad out of my backpack and carefully type in the web address to the browser. Much to my shock, Joe and Brody are the stars of the video which pops up. It looks like Joe filmed them watching sign language videos and attempting to replicate them. The video is captioned **Love comes in many languages.**

I watch the video three more times before Heather comes over and delivers my sticky bun. "What in the world are you watching? You look like you're about to cry."

"I am," I admit as I position the iPad so Heather can see what I've been watching.

"Oh my heavens! That's about the sweetest thing I've ever seen. Boy, Joe has really embraced this whole sign language thing, hasn't he?"

"It would appear he is more open to it than he has been, that's for sure."

"What an amazing caption. Is that a special message for you?" Heather says as she sits down and watches the video one more time.

"I don't know for sure, but I suspect it is. I told Joe that if he truly wanted to understand Brody, he had to learn the way Brody speaks — even if it's different from the hopes and dreams he had for Brody. Amazingly, he seems to have listened."

"Things not going so well between you?"

"Let's just say Joe has a hard time accepting change. Well, change and help — if the help means he has to change."

"Honey, that's pretty much the life story of almost every guy I know," Heather answers with a laugh. "Sometimes, you just have to take their hand and lead them through it so they can understand that not all change is bad."

"You might be right. It looks like at least some of my questions are getting answered. Maybe it's time for me to accept a little change too."

CHAPTER NINE

JOE

I CAN TELL FROM my website counter that someone is viewing our video over and over. If I posted it correctly, Brynley should be the only one who has the link. I am too antsy to wait patiently for her response. Typing carefully on my phone — these buttons are not made for big hands — I ask, "So, what do you think? Did you like it?"

As I wait for her response, I try to mentally review the signs we've been practicing. Some signs make perfect logical sense, others not so much. Even so, Brody seems to be having a great time learning them. I'm pretty sure he called me a silly goose the other day. He cackled with joy when he saw my expression. That's the most beautiful sound on the planet.

My phone vibrates in my hand and I look down with trepidation. I smile when I read, "That was the most beautiful thing I've ever seen in my whole life. You are amazing! Thank you so much for sharing."

Growing frustrated with email, I pull up the phone app and call Brynley.

She sounds a little startled when she answers, "Hello?"

"Hey, it's Joe. I'm glad you liked our video. I wanted you to see tangible proof that my heart and mind are open to change. I haven't had to share Brody in a long time and it's going to take some getting used to, but I promise to try to work with you to help Brody instead of against you."

"I got your message loud and clear, Joe," Brynley replies. She hesitates before she adds, "I'm willing to come back for now. But I don't know how long I can stay. Very soon, I'll have a new job and I don't know how I'm going to balance everything."

"Okay, I understand. No pressure, I promise. You can stay in the guest room. I miss you so much. Having you here even for a short time is better than not at all."

"I've missed you guys even more than I miss my family." Brynley's voice cracks, "and I miss my family a bunch."

"Come home," I coax. "My previous offer still stands. Brody and I will be waiting for you with warm hugs, hot chocolate, and chicken soup."

"That's the best offer I've had in forever. I'll be there after work, I promise."

My heart soars at her words. "Brynley, just so you know you've made my day — maybe even my whole year. I'm glad you gave us a chance to start over."

As I hang up the phone, I throw a fist pump in the air. For a guy who has been a confirmed bachelor for several years, I am ridiculously happy to be having my roommate back, even if it is just temporarily.

I start to run into the front room to share my glorious news with Brody. But I stop dead in my tracks. Something tells me this will be a wonderful surprise.

I watch from the kitchen table as Brynley rushes Brody out the front door as if she has done it every single day of his life. The woman is beyond remarkable. I'm incredibly lucky she even came back after my epic whine-fest the other day. I don't know what came over me.

Sometime during the past lonely, torturous weeks, it occurred to me that instead of feeling bad about her connection with my son, I ought to say a prayer of thanks and learn everything I possibly can before she decides I'm a big schmuck. Something tells me as painful as my split from Kara-Jane was, it's going to hurt a lot more if Brynley ever decides to leave for good.

Despite our rocky start, she's settled back into taking care of every need Brody and I have.

Well … maybe not *every* need.

But our relationship isn't there yet. I'm not sure exactly when I started thinking in terms of our relationship. Maybe it was when she insisted on running a bubble bath for me and dried my hair so I wouldn't get chilled. Or, maybe it was when she was teaching Brody all the names of his favorite dinosaurs in sign language and gently holding his hand to show him how to fingerspell words he doesn't know in sign language. Maybe, it was when she was laughing out loud at Tom and Jerry cartoons as we ate Cocoa Puffs with chocolate milk and read the comics in the newspaper.

Whatever it is, we click in a big way.

Even with all of my stupid insecurities about my inability to communicate with Brody, I've discovered a powerful need for Brynley that can't be denied. Not just for Brody — although that would be amazing. I've decided I need Brynley almost as much as the air I breathe.

My fingers are itching to write her a love song.

Unfortunately, after Brynley discovered me trying to sing with my raw, sore throat, she banned me from the guitar for a few days. She insists I need to fully rest my voice. She's not wrong, but it's totally frustrating.

Sighing, I turn the television on and flip through the channels to find a game. It's funny, I've been juggling two careers for a while together with being a single parent. I used to think that if I got more rest, things would be so much easier. I never expected to get to the point where I'm tired of resting.

When Brynley returns after dropping Brody off at school, she is carrying a couple of boxes. I rush to grab the boxes from her hands. As I grab the heavy boxes, I ask, "What's all this? It's not Halloween yet, so bobbing for apples seems like an unlikely choice."

"My gosh, that's a great idea! We should do that for Halloween. I have a recipe for awesome caramel apples too. These are apples and pears. My friend can't sell them because they aren't perfect, and she's sick of applesauce and fritters. She begged me to take them off of her hands."

I raise an eyebrow. "Brody can take a few in his lunch, but what are we going to do with the rest?" I motion toward the large box.

Brynley grins at me. "Never fear, I have plans for those."

I wrinkle my nose. "Brody doesn't really like applesauce, and to be honest, I'm not big on it either."

Brynley grimaces. "Yeah, I found that out the hard way. I thought Brody was going to throw up."

"It's a texture thing for him," I explain. "Or at least that's what I think it is."

"Maybe. But, your son goes through boxes of fruit leather. So, I'm going to teach him to make his own."

I glance at the boxes skeptically. "Sounds complicated."

"It's not, I swear!" Brynley starts to pick up a box and carry it over to the sink.

I jump up to move the boxes for her. She scowls at me. "You're supposed to be resting."

"I'm sick and tired of 'resting'. Besides, this is nothing. The new antibiotics have started to kick in. I'm feeling almost human."

"Umm-hmm, too bad for you."

"What?" I ask incredulously. "I thought you'd be overjoyed that I feel better."

"Oh, trust me I am. You just chose a really bad time to reveal it. Brody and I are going to need lots of help peeling fruit — " Brynley winks at me and starts looking around the kitchen. "You have a food processor around here?"

"Why? Do we need one?"

"Technically, no. But it would make things much easier."

"Gotcha. It's right in front of you."

Brynley starts searching through the things on my counter. "Are you sure? I don't see anything here."

I step up behind her and reach over her head. "That's because you're not looking high enough."

As soon as I start speaking, Brynley spins around

with her hand on her chest. "Geez, you scared the daylights out of me!"

She looks a little shaky, so I place my hands on her waist to steady her. Instinctively, she puts her hands on my chest.

The pose seems so natural it takes my breath away. As a tall, lanky guy, I usually tower over women. Once again, I'm amazed Brynley fits in my arms like she was meant to be there.

"Mmm, this is nice," Brynley murmurs. "It's too bad you're sick. The thoughts running through my head have nothing to do with helping you get better."

I lean down and brush a kiss across her cheek. "I don't know about that. I've heard kissing releases all sorts of endorphins and those are very healing."

"That's a good theory. Should we test it out?"

"I don't want to get you sick — "

"You said you're almost finished with your antibiotics. Besides, I've been cuddled up next to you watching game shows and movies for several days since I came back. Any cross-contamination of germs would've happened a long time ago." Brynley stands on her tiptoes and kisses me lightly.

I groan and pull her closer to deepen the kiss. After I pull away, I murmur, "That's the best medicine I've had in forever."

"Me too, Joe. Me too. I'm not even sick, but I feel so much better," Brynley whispers before she captures my face in her hands and pulls me toward her for a very thorough kiss.

Brynley helps Brody off with his coat and hangs up his backpack. "Any homework tonight?"

Brody shakes his head and makes a sign.

Brynley grins at his response. "Oh, you're all done? Great job!"

Brody walks over to the big apples and pears we washed. He starts pulling them out of the bowl and lining them up. He looks up at Brynley and makes the sign for apple. Then he pulls a pear out of the bowl and looks up at Brynley.

"That's a pear," she explains while she signs the name of the fruit.

Brody picks up the pear and pretends to eat it. Then he glances over at me as if he is seeking permission. Taking a cue from Brynley, I try to sign as I speak, "Yes, you can eat the pear." I get stuck on the word eat.

So, Brynley repeats my sentence and shows us both the sign for eat.

Brody runs over to the refrigerator and pulls out one of his favorite snacks. He shows it to Brynley and makes the sign for eat.

Brynley's brows furrow. "Okay, that one's a little tricky. This is the sign for cheese," she answers as she makes a grinding motion with her palms. "I'm sorry, I don't know the sign for string. The sign for white is this," Brynley says as she demonstrates the sign.

"That's perfect for you, Brody. You love string cheese, so if you call it white cheese, it looks like you're showing your love of string cheese."

Brody nods. He grins at both of us before he signs eat, apple, white cheese, and something else I don't recognize.

Brynley chuckles. "You and your chocolate milk. I thought I loved chocolate milk, but you have me beat by a mile. Go wash your hands and I'll get your snack."

Brody runs from the room and Scout chases after him.

Abruptly, I sink down into one of the kitchen chairs. Alarmed, Brynley gasps. "I knew you should have taken it easy. You've been up too long."

Mutely, I shake my head.

"What's wrong?" Brynley presses.

"It's not what's wrong that's bothering me, it's what's right. You know, that's the first time I've had a conversation with Brody since he was a baby. It doesn't even matter that we were talking about snack food. He just told us what he wanted. I can't thank you enough. Because of you, I'm going to be able to talk to my son."

Brynley wipes a tear off my cheek. "It's the least I can do. I'm just sad my new job starts in three weeks. I'll do my best to teach him as many words as I can before I have to go."

"Do you really have to go?" I blurt before I can think better of it. "You just got back. I'm sorry I wasted all those days because I was butt-hurt."

The expression in Brynley's eyes is bleak. "I think I will. I have to start my practicum with the county, and I'd like to continue working with Locate My Heart. I won't have much spare time."

She wraps her arms around her middle and looks out the window. "I didn't realize how much I missed having family around until you guys came into my life. I love being here with you guys. I didn't realize how lonely I was until I had to go back home to my apartment life.

It's going to be hard to go back to being alone."

"Then don't," I say throwing caution to the wind.

Brynley's eyebrows raise. "Do you realize what you're asking?"

"I do. I can't believe I'm saying this after all the garbage Kara-Jane put me through — but I don't ever want you to leave again."

Brynley studies me for a moment before she asks, "Are you asking me to stay for yourself or for Brody?"

"I could tell you it's only for Brody's well-being. But that wouldn't be the truth. I want you to stay because I care about you — far more than I expected to. You've made my world a happier place. If this is a dream, I don't want to wake up."

"This is the stuff fairytales are made of, for sure. Honestly, that's part of my hesitation. What if this is too good to be true? I mean, if we had met a couple aisles over, we would be the perfect cliché."

I look at her blankly.

The corner of her mouth lifts up in a crooked grin. "You don't watch many chick flicks, do you? Many of them start with a beautiful couple bonding over produce in the grocery store."

I pick up a pear and an apple from the bowl in the center of the kitchen table. "We got the produce part covered, any other objections?"

"This thing — whatever it is — between us is happening so fast, I don't know what to think. I'm a little scared. What if I overstep my bounds again and make you feel uncomfortable? I don't want to feel like I'm walking on eggshells."

I stand up, walk over to her and gather her into a loose embrace. "I'm scared too. Relationships haven't worked out so well for me. But, I learned some lessons from the last time I was an idiot. I'll try not to make the same mistake."

"What about Brody?" Brynley whispers into my chest.

"I don't think he's going to object. After all, he's the one who found you and brought you into our lives. Since you came back, I've never seen him so happy."

"What happens when I have to leave again?"

"I hope that day never comes," I admit.

Brynley looks up at me with a desolate expression on her face. "People always leave. That's the way life goes."

"Maybe we can learn from our mistakes and change the rules," I whisper before I capture her lips in a passionate kiss.

CHAPTER TEN

BRYNLEY

KENDALL GLANCES OVER AT me as she stirs her cinnamon tea. "You haven't been around much. Is everything okay.?"

I blush to the roots of my hair. "Umm … everything is fine, why do you ask?"

"Well, you're missing your usual spark and even when you're here, I get the feeling your mind is somewhere else."

"That's because it is," I admit. "Things are not so fine with me. I'm trying to figure out what to do with my life. I'm starting a new job in a few weeks and my love life is like a roller coaster. Some days I think it'd be easier just to be single again."

"Speaking of your love life, how in the world have you and Joe kept the paparazzi out of your business?"

"Luck, I guess. Maybe they think I'm one of Brody's therapists or something. Joe has been too sick to leave the house for a few weeks. He's trying to get better before they go on tour."

"What does he do with Brody when he's on tour?"

I slump back in my office chair. "That's a really good question. Things have been so crazy, I haven't even asked him that. Maybe that's why he asked me to move in. You know, suddenly, his question makes a lot more sense now."

Kendall walks over and puts her hand on my shoulder. "Don't look so glum. Joe has been touring for a long time — long before you met him. I'm sure he has this all worked out."

I look up at my boss, with a pained expression. "What if I misread this whole situation and the only thing Joe is looking for is a qualified nanny? Maybe that's why he was so insistent that I come back."

Kendall chuckles. "Oh honey, if a nanny was what Joe was looking for, he would have women lined up around the block. As we discussed, he is one sexy guy. He doesn't have to look hard for people willing to hang around."

I wrinkle my nose. "You're kidding! People would really use Brody to get to Joe?"

"I don't do much with the security side of things, but I've heard Jameson talk with Tristan and Logan. Sometimes fans will stoop to unprecedented lows to work their way into the lives of someone famous."

"That's despicable! No wonder Joe finds it hard to trust anyone."

"It would be hard to be in his shoes. The way I understand it, Brody is a challenging child and people could take advantage of that."

"Challenging? That's not the way I see Brody. He's bright, funny, and obsessed with dinosaurs just like any other five-year-old."

"Oh, I must've misunderstood what I heard. I was

under the impression that Brody doesn't talk or really relate to anyone other than his dad."

"That's just not true," I argue defensively. "He may not talk, but he communicates clearly and he's learning sign language as fast as I can teach him the signs. He is phenomenal."

"I wonder why he didn't teach Brody sign language before since he works with Tara and Aidan?"

"Some specialist somewhere told Joe that introducing sign language would be a crutch and discourage Brody from being vocal. I think the dude was entirely wrong. Brody has tons to say, he just needs to figure out the best way to do it."

"That's the passionate Brynley I know. But I have to ask, are you falling in love with Brody or Joe?"

I get up and walk over toward the coffee machine. "Why do I have to choose? Can't it be both?"

"It absolutely can be. I just want you to think about it because I once thought a child could fix everything in my relationship. I was wrong. Please make sure you're not putting that kind of burden on Brody."

"I know it looks that way from the outside, but trust me, I am every bit as attached to Joe as I am to Brody. It's hard for me to imagine one without the other, but even if Joe wasn't a parent, he's my kind of guy. He's sweet, thoughtful, artistic, and honest to a fault — even when he has messed up. I still wonder what he sees in me, but I'm quickly falling head over heels."

"Make sure you tell Joe that loud and clear. If he's anything like the guys in my life, he'll find a dozen ways to get that all tangled in his head."

"I understand. It's pretty tangled in my head too. He asked me to move in with him. I don't know what to say.

He's already asked me to leave once. I don't know if I can trust what's between us."

"Understood. Relationships are scary."

"I never expected my path in life would include falling in love with a famous star. But then again, if life went the way other people planned my life, I'd be celebrating my tenth wedding anniversary soon and probably have a passel of kids."

Kendall comes over and puts her arm around my shoulders. "I don't have all the sage advice of the Girlfriend Posse, but I think before you decide, you need to figure out exactly why he wants you there. If you don't figure that out first, you'll always wonder."

"Maybe I'm afraid to find out," I admit with a sigh. "These last few weeks have been magical. I'm not sure I want reality to interfere with my fairytale."

"I know the hard times seem like they are interrupting your fairytale. But what they're really doing is making you stronger so that when the good times come around, you can relish your happiness."

"You sound like Will. Ever since your brother found Mariam, he keeps telling me I need to listen to my heart and figure out what my heart wish is. Speaking of heart wishes, I wonder when Will and Mariam are going to get married?"

Kendall grabs my hand and pulls me into her office. I'm taken aback when she closes her door.

"Oh my gosh! Don't tell me those two split up. They're perfect for each other."

Kendall shakes her head. "Thank heavens, that's not it. I can't believe Will didn't talk to you about this. I thought he messaged everybody."

I smack my forehead with my hand. "I forgot to tell

him that my cell phone bit the dust. I'm using an old-style flip phone and I don't have the messaging set up on it. Why? What was Will supposed to tell me?"

"Oh boy, don't tell Will your phone is broken, he'll buy you the latest version and feel compelled to invent accessories to go with it." Kendall lowers her voice. "Anyway, you know that bar Aidan and Tara like to go to? Sawdust & Horseshoes or something like that — "

I nod. "Remember, we went to Elijah's birthday party there?"

"Oh that's right. I forgot about that. My brother being the closet romantic he is decided that rather than stressing Mariam out with tons of wedding prep, he is going to surprise her with a wedding ceremony. Aidan rented out the whole joint to have a Thanksgiving feast and the wedding will be afterward."

"Your brother is either very brave or very stupid. How do you think Mariam will handle this? She likes to be in charge of things and keep them organized. Come to think about it, they work together. So, how is your brother keeping this under wraps?"

"Two words: Girlfriend Posse. Let's just say my brother has suddenly developed an affinity for fishing."

"Fishing?" I ask, feeling lost.

Kendall laughs out loud. "They're not really going fishing. It just gives Will an excuse to go over to Denny's house where the wedding squad meets to work out the details."

"I understand his approach for the little stuff, but how is Mariam getting her dress?"

"That's where Jordan comes in. Remember the beautiful bridesmaids dresses she made for my wedding? She has all of Mariam's measurements from then. While

Mariam and I were discussing ideas from my dress, Will was quietly taking notes about what Mariam would like to see in her own dress. My brother helped design his bride's dress. It's weirdly romantic, isn't it?"

"I just hope Mariam isn't superstitious."

"Oh, that's the beauty of this. Jordan is keeping the final product secret from even my brother. He has a vague idea what it will look like because he helped develop the sketches, but as you know with Jordan's work, the sketches don't do her garments justice."

"That's genius! I bet Will is completely fit to be tied. Obviously, as his twin, you will be there, but who else is in the wedding party?"

Kendall shoots me a surprised glance. "You are. You know Will considers you one of his best friends?"

"He does? How odd. I think he's cool and we dated a few times and hung out while he was trying to figure out how to court Mariam, but I don't know if that makes me his best friend."

"That's funny, to hear my brother tell it, you are the one who encouraged him to be himself with Mariam."

"So, I know Will doesn't do anything in a small way. Who else is in the wedding?"

"Well, besides you, there's Jameson and me, Toby and Pauline, Aidan and Tara, with Elijah and Mindy as best man and matron of honor."

I clear my throat. "Well, this is a tad awkward. The last time we did this, I walked up the aisle with Toby. I don't think Pauline would like that much. Who am I supposed to walk with?"

Kendall blows her bangs out of her eyes. "Not to freak you out or anything, but when I asked Mindy that the other day, she said to tell you, 'Your heart will know the answer'."

I sink down onto the couch in Kendall's office as my knees grow weak.

"So, she thinks I should ask a guy I've been seeing for just a few weeks to walk down the aisle with me at my friend's wedding? If I do that, Joe may just ask me to leave again."

Kendall rolls her eyes. "I doubt that very much. Be honest, is that what your heart is telling you?" Kendall presses me.

I sigh wistfully. "Yeah, I think it is. I have been hanging around in sweats. It's about time Joe sees the womanly side of me."

Kendall grins widely. "See? That wasn't so hard. I think Joe might actually be your heart wish."

I groan. "Remind me again how your goofy brother defines heart wish?"

"A heart wish is something or someone who makes you so happy you can't imagine life without them in it."

I swallow hard. "If Joe Summers isn't my heart wish, he's awfully darn close."

Kendall smiles gently. "Well, there you go. I guess you better make plans for Thanksgiving with Joe. Make sure you remind him that all of this is hush-hush. I don't want to be responsible for ruining my brother's surprise."

CHAPTER ELEVEN

JOE

THE MOVIE CREDITS ROLL on the Disney movie we were watching with Brody. He is sacked out with his head on Brynley's lap and his feet draping over mine. I stretch out my arms and gingerly scoot out from under Brody's feet. "I'll take him to bed. Good call on making him dress in his PJs and brush his teeth before we started the movie."

Brynley shrugs. "I have lots of siblings and cousins. I've done more than my fair share of babysitting in my life." After I lift Brody up and start to move toward the stairs, Brynley grabs his blanket and favorite stuffed animal. "We can't forget Bun-Bun," she whispers as she follows me up the stairs.

I gently set Brody down in bed and kiss his cheek. "Love you to the moon and back, Brody." I cover him up with his blanket and place his stuffed animal next to him.

He sighs and curls up with Bun-Bun. Brynley comes over to his bed and pulls the blanket up over his shoulders and brushes her fingers through his hair. "Sweet dreams."

Quietly, Brynley and I tiptoe out of Brody's room and close the door behind us. As we hit the top of the stairs, I say, "Now that my voice is back, I need to start working on our set for the tour."

A fleeting look of panic passes over Brynley's face. "Umm … do you have a few minutes to talk?"

My heart skips a few beats. "Now, what did I do? Nothing good flows from a conversation which starts like that —"

Brynley reaches out and puts her hand on my forearm. "It's nothing awful. I just have some questions for you."

"Okay, let me grab my guitar and I'll be down."

• • •

Brynley has discovered I like chocolate almost as much as my son. As soon as I sit down on the couch, she brings me some hot chocolate with marshmallows.

"Do you need anything else while I'm up?" Brynley asks.

"You could bring me some of those fruit thingies we made. I'll admit, I was skeptical at first. But they're totally addicting."

"Don't worry, we'll make some more. Brody had so much fun helping us. He's really coordinated for his age. I actually think he's better with the vegetable peeler than I am."

"Yeah, I couldn't believe he was so jazzed about peeling apples and pears."

Brynley hands me a handful of fruit leather-wrapped in parchment paper. "I'm surprised these even finished cooking since Brody kept opening the oven to check on their progress. The next time we make these, I'll time it so they cook overnight. I can't wait until strawberries are in season."

I pat the couch beside me. "So, don't keep me in suspense any longer. What do we need to discuss? I hope I haven't chased you away again."

Brynley bites her lip and sits on the couch with her legs under her. "Not so far. I just have some questions. Umm ... What happens to Brody when you go on tour? You guys are leaving in a couple weeks, right? Is that why you want me to move in?"

"No! I want you to move in with us because I like you. I like you a lot. With you, I don't have to worry about being 'on' or presenting myself as this perfect up-and-coming music star. You take the time to listen to me. You don't judge me for my reactions to things which make my soul hurt. With you, I can just be me — as flawed as I am. You even forgave me when I almost blew up our entire relationship. As crazy as it sounds, you make me feel content and settled. There is something about us that feels like we are meant to be. It's like you've taken up residence in my heart and I don't want to let you go."

"Wow! I feel stupid now. I mean, we've been having a great time together and, to be honest, this feels more like my home than my own apartment. I watched all my friends fall in love and I was beginning to wonder what was wrong with me. Turns out nothing is wrong with me, my heart was just waiting for yours. Kendall asked me today if I was falling in love with Brody instead of you."

I pin her with a level gaze. "Well, are you?" My heartbeat thunders in my ears as I wait for her answer. It's funny how Kendall gave voice to my deepest fear even though she doesn't know me all that well.

"It's true that Brody's distress was what drew my attention. I wanted to turn his day around and put a smile on his face. I adore your son."

I flinch. "Why do I feel like there is a but at the end of that sentence?"

Brynley shakes her head vehemently. "No but, just an and. *And* then I fell hard for Brody's daddy."

"I'm thrilled to hear that. Things have not always been perfect between us, but I'm glad you came back."

"I am too. You're not anything like I expected. When I finally figured out who you were, I thought I knew what famous people were like. I was wrong. I didn't find a vain, spoiled superstar. Instead, I found a father who loves his son more than the air he breathes, even though sometimes it's hard. I found someone who, despite the fact that it's painful, allows me to bond with his son so I can help him learn to communicate better. I found a kind and generous man who cheers me on when I talk about my hopes, dreams and aspirations. I still can't get over the fact that we found each other in the most awkward, clichéd situation ever. Yet, it seems like we've always been destined to be together."

I swallow hard and have to clear my throat. "I thought it was just me. I don't know about you, but it feels to me like we're already a family."

"Exactly. I feel the same way, but after our earlier misunderstanding, I just had to check with you to make sure I was reading the situation correctly."

"You are reading things just right. To get back to your original question, when I go on tour, Brody stays with a lovely retired teacher. Mrs. Northrup is the grandmother Brody never had. She picks him up from school and he stays with her overnight. Since Aidan and Tara adopted Maddie, he tries to keep the tours short during the school year. This time, it's only an eight-day swing through the southern states."

"I feel silly saying this, but I'm going to be lost without you guys for eight days."

"I'm going to miss you too, but at least I know you'll be here when I get home. I'll talk to Mrs. Northrup and maybe you all can get together a couple times. Perhaps Joyce would like to learn some sign language to reinforce what we've been doing here at the house."

"I'd love that. I just want Brody to be happy. I'm glad I don't have to feel guilty about working while you're gone. I was worried about what would happen to my buddy."

"Brody will be safe, I promise. So, what was your other question?"

"What are you and Brody doing for Thanksgiving?"

I cringe. "I have to do a private gig with Aidan and Mindy that day. I'm sorry, I can't tell you anything about it because it's supposed to be a big secret."

Brynley giggles at the expression on my face. "Relax. I'm in on the secret. I would've been in-the-know earlier, except my phone broke and I never got Will's text message. But I'm all on board now. That's why I asked you."

"You're going to Will's wedding? I thought you told me you guys went out for a while."

Brynley reaches out for my hand. "We did. But we had zero chemistry as a couple. He is an awesome friend. I admire everything he does with his company and his charity, but he wasn't the guy for me. I'm thrilled that he and Mariam fell in love."

"He probably thinks you're pretty awesome too. Not very many women would be so generous."

"He told Kendall he considers me to be one of his

best friends and he swears I'm the reason he felt brave enough to show Mariam who he really was. I don't know if I did anything spectacular except to be his friend. Anyway, he asked me to be one of the bridesmaids. When I was in Kendall's wedding, Toby was my groomsman. He has another partner this year. Have you seen them? He and Pauline are so cute together."

"So, you're asking me to put on a monkey suit and escort you down the aisle at your best friend's wedding?"

Brynley blushes a deep shade of red. "Yeah, I totally forgot about the paparazzi. Maybe it's not such a good idea."

"From what I understand, Aidan goes to great lengths to make sure Sawdust & Horseshoes is a paparazzi-free zone. I think it'll be safe. I would be honored to be your date."

Brynley rewards me with a wide smile. "See? Conversations that start with 'I need to talk to you' aren't necessarily all evil."

"Some of them are. But I'm glad we had this conversation. I need you to know, even though Brody is happier when you're here, he is not the reason I want you to stick around. I like you, Brynley Summer Meeker — because you are smart and beautiful inside and out. I can't wait until we officially have our first date that doesn't involve a G rated movie and popcorn."

"I understand the Girlfriend Posse is planning this little shindig. Something like that is entirely within the realm of possibility."

"True enough. But even if it is, I'll have the time of my life because you'll be there with me."

Chapter Twelve

Brynley

Heather sets a chocolate filled croissant down in front of me and refills my cup of coffee. "Is everything okay? You've been staring out into space for several minutes."

I turn my attention to her and blush a little. "Just thinking about something."

"Something or someone? Or maybe I should say someones?" Heather asks pointedly.

My eyes widen. "I forgot you know about Joe," I whisper. "I wasn't sure I could tell anyone without risking his reputation in the media."

"P'shaw! Why would you worry about something like that? You have made a career out of helping people and you're getting your Master's degree! Not many people, including me, can say that."

"You don't think the paparazzi will have a field day with the fact that we just met and I'm already living at his house? It's only been a few months."

"I saw that beautiful video he sent you a while back, remember? It sure seems like you're more than just a fling to Joe."

My cheeks flush and turn hot. "I hope so. It feels like we've been through an awful lot of ups and downs. Still, I'm not sure what the public is going to think about our relationship. We are moving sort of fast."

"I understand you've been dating Joe since the summer, right? By the standards of this group, you guys have been dating forever," Heather winks. "After all, Halloween is tomorrow."

"Oh … I wasn't aware everyone knows."

"Take a deep breath. It just came up in conversation. William and Isobel came over from the coast to visit with Denny and Gwendolyn. Not long ago, they were all in here having coffee and pastries with Kiera and Jeff. Joe was at the next table studying lyrics. He overheard Gwendolyn say something to Isobel about being a teacher. So, he explained how you guys have been working with Brody to teach him sign language. Of course, people had questions, so he confirmed that you guys are a couple."

"What did Isobel think of our sign language experiment? It didn't seem to go over so well with Joe in the beginning. Although, he seems on board now, as you saw in the video."

"Well, I wasn't there for the whole conversation, but I know they were talking about buying Brody some picture books to help expand his vocabulary. Isobel thought your plan to introduce sign language was brilliant."

"That's a phenomenal idea. I remember a great word book I used to read my nieces and nephews when they were learning to talk. I'll have to look for it. Don't mention Halloween to me. I miss hanging out with Brody since Joe is gone. I can't believe Brody is going to miss it."

"Doesn't Brody want to go? I know Maddie has been driving Aidan and Tara crazy because she keeps changing her mind about what she wants to be."

"I don't think he is going to go trick or treating. Brody isn't staying with me because I have to work. Joe made arrangements with his usual babysitter. I haven't seen Brody in four days. It's hard to miss both of them so much."

"Well, why don't you offer to take him? I don't know Mrs. Northrup very well, but she does come in for my Yule logs during the holidays. Last time I saw her, she seemed to be having a little trouble getting around. She might welcome the help."

"You don't think I'd be imposing?" I ask, trying not to sound too hopeful.

"Nah, impose away. Halloween is fun!" Heather answers with a grin. "Now, tell me what it's like to date the mysterious Joe Summers," she adds with a conspiratorial grin.

"Confusing," I blurt.

"That's how it is for everyone. In the beginning, Ty was so hot and cold with me my head spun. Eventually, it all works out."

"I never expected to date anyone like Joe Summers. You know what he did before he went on tour?"

Heather leans closer.

"He got a sitter for Brody and he took me up in the mountains to this beautiful clearing. Then, he set up an amazing picnic with all my favorite foods."

"Oh, how romantic! The quiet, shy guys can be dangerous — or at least that's what my sister says."

"You don't know the meaning of the word romantic until Joe Summers gives you an up-close and personal concert of all your favorite songs. I thought I was going to melt into a little puddle right there on the stump."

"Oh honey, I get it. Even just being in the audience when Joe sings his ballads is heart-stopping enough. I can't imagine what it would be like if he was singing love songs directly to you."

"It was magical. I've never experienced anything like that," I confess.

"So, why is it confusing?"

"Joe Summers is a huge star. He could have any woman in the world. Why would he settle for me? It all seems too good to be true."

"Why would he like you? You are smart, beautiful and spunky. Guys love a woman with a little spunk."

"I guess I don't see myself that way. I see the young woman who was shunned by her family because she wasn't good enough to live up to their expectations. I see the woman who lives paycheck to paycheck and sometimes comes up short. I see the woman with mountains of student debt and no paying job on the horizon. I'm afraid Joe is going to wake up one day and see the woman I see and change his mind again."

"I understand. It's hard to overcome the messages our families stamped on our heart. But you're not defined by your family's opinion of you. Look how much you've grown and changed without their help. You need to have faith that the woman Joe sees when he looks at you exists under all your fear and doubt."

Taking a deep breath, I call the number Joe left for me.

She picks it up on the third ring, just as I am about to give up and decide it was a bad idea to call.

"Hello? If this is a telephone solicitor, I'm not interested in whatever you're selling me."

"No, Mrs. Northrup, I'm not a telephone solicitor. I am Brynley Meeker. I've been staying with Joe and Brody. I wondered if it would be okay if I take Brody trick-or-treating tonight?"

"Oh dear! I'm not sure Brody has a costume. He might not understand how trick-or-treating works. It could be hard for a child like him."

"It's all right. I can take care of all that. I just thought it would be fun for him to go."

"Well, Mr. Summers said Brody was free to go with you any time. I'm not sure how to help him. He has been very sad. I've never seen him like this — but maybe this will cheer him up. Do you want to keep him overnight in case you are out late? I go to bed mighty early these days."

"If you don't mind, I'd love that. I'll be there in a few minutes." It's all I can do not to throw cartwheels when I hang up the phone. I haven't been this excited about trick-or-treat since I was about eight years old.

Stopping to pet Scout and dump a scoop of food in his bowl, I make my way to Joe's guest room where I've been staying. I stand on my tiptoes to unearth something I bought for Brody before I knew exactly when Joe was going to be gone on his tour. Even though I'm the only living being in the house except for Scout, I grin from ear-to-ear and do a little jig. Brody is going to be so excited!

———•———

"I am so glad you're here," Mrs. Northrup says as she

opens her front door. "Usually, Brody is content to color and watch movies when he stays at my house. Something's different this time. I can't seem to make him happy — even with his favorite foods."

"I'm sorry Brody is distressed. Maybe I can help figure out what's wrong."

"Good luck with that. I don't see how it's —"

As soon Brody hears my voice, he comes barreling toward me and hugs my leg.

"Oh my heavens, I've never seen Brody do anything of the sort — even with his father. What a miracle!"

When I look down, I notice Brody's face is tear-stained. I squat down and sign as I speak, "What's wrong?"

Brody makes my name sign and then signs no and points around the room. He points to himself and then signs the word scared.

My heart breaks in two as I sign and voice, "I'm sorry, buddy. I have to work during the day. I didn't mean to make you scared."

Mrs. Northrup is watching our conversation intently. "Well, isn't that something? I thought Mr. Summers didn't want Brody to use sign language."

"Originally, that was his intent. However, I didn't know that when I first met them, so I taught Brody some signs. Brody has a remarkable affinity for sign language. He has expanded his vocabulary a great deal in just a short period of time. Brody just told me he was scared. I understand, he probably worried I wasn't coming back. Joe asked me to leave once before and Brody didn't handle it well."

"I'm not sure it's a good idea to allow Brody to take the lazy route. He needs to learn to speak."

"Sign language allows Brody to communicate effectively. It is a language all of its own. It's not second-best to verbal expression, it's just different."

"With all due respect, I am the teacher here."

"That might be true, but you had no idea what was wrong with Brody until I was able to ask him and get an answer." I turn to Brody and ask, "Are you ready to go trick-or-treating?"

He looks up at me and signs cracker.

"You might get crackers, but I think you'll probably get candy. That's what most people give out."

Brody grins widely. He points to himself and then signs the word candy and rubs his tummy.

"Okay, you can eat some candy, but first you have to ask for it." I show him the sign as I say, "You knock on someone's door and when they answer, you say, 'trick or treat'. Then, after they give you candy, you have to be sure to say, 'thank you'."

Brody tries to mimic the sign with one hand.

"You need two hands to sign trick-or-treat. So, you'll have to set your candy bucket down before you knock on the door. Would you like to wear a costume?"

Brody looks puzzled.

I reach down and pull items from the tote bag sitting at my feet. "Would you like to be a dinosaur or a lion?" I ask as I show him the two packages.

His response requires no interpretation. He snatches the dinosaur costume right out of my hand and starts to shed his clothes.

"Wait!" I say as I sign. "This is Oregon, you need to leave your clothes on under your costume."

He stops with one arm out of his shirt. He shrugs

and pokes his arm back through the armhole. I help him take the dinosaur costume out of the package and put it on. "Oh shoot, I wish I hadn't broken my cell phone. I would love to take a picture of you. You look ferocious!"

"I have to admit, he looks quite imposing," Mrs. Northrup says. "I'd be happy to take Brody's picture with my phone and send it to his father."

"What do you say, Brody? You want your dad to see a picture of you all dressed up as a dinosaur?"

Brody nods vigorously.

"Okay, what do you tell Mrs. Northrup?"

Brody turns to his babysitter and shyly signs, "Thank you."

"You're very welcome, young man. Let me go get my cell phone. In the meantime, you can practice how to ask me for candy," Mrs. Northrup says as she turns to leave the room.

"You look most awesome," I remark as I straighten his dinosaur head-piece.

Brody looks anxious as he waits for Mrs. Northrup to return. When she rounds the corner carrying a cell phone and a bowl of candy, he grins.

"First, I want to get a picture of you and then I'd like you to pose with Brynley. Something tells me your dad would like to see both of you."

Brody stands statue-still as Mrs. Northrup takes his picture.

I squat down beside Brody and she takes some more pictures. As I stand up, I notice Brody sign, "Thank you."

"I like those manners, Brody. Good manners will take you far. Would you like some candy?"

Brody nods enthusiastically.

"What do you say?" Mrs. Northrup prompts.

Brody glances over to me for reassurance before he signs, "Trick-or-treat!"

I hand Brody a bright orange bag from my tote bag. He approaches Mrs. Northrup tentatively and she places a handful of candy in his bag. When he sees what she placed in there, his eyes widen and he starts to giggle.

"That's fun, isn't it? You did it perfectly. Now, what do you tell Mrs. Northrup?"

He looks up at her and signs, "Thank you!" This time, he has an ear-to-ear grin. He turns around and looks at me and signs, "Go please?"

I start to interpret his question, but Mrs. Northrup holds up her hand. "No translation needed. I'll let you guys get on your way. Have fun, Brody. It's great to see you smile."

CHAPTER THIRTEEN

JOE

MY HEART PLUMMETS TO my toes when I see I missed an email from Mrs. Northrup. I hope everything is all right with Brody. For some reason, leaving on this tour seemed so much harder than it's been before. For the first time since I started working for Aidan O'Brien, I felt tempted to say, "Screw it all!" and just stay home with Brody and Brynley.

Sighing, I click on the email. I draw in a surprised breath when I see Brody dressed in a dinosaur costume with a big grin on his face. The next picture makes my heart beat a little faster. I should've known Brynley was responsible for the look on Brody's face. It's impossible not to smile when she's around. I can't believe I almost threw it all away.

There is a note attached from Mrs. Northrup, which reads, "Your new girlfriend is pretty special. She cares a great deal for Brody. It's obvious the feeling is mutual."

Fighting back tears, I study the pictures of my beautiful son.

I jump when Aidan slides into the bus seat next to

mine and accidentally shut my computer screen. "Not bad news, I hope?" Aidan asks as he points to my computer.

I shake my head. "No, it's the opposite. Look — " I open my computer screen and show him the pictures.

"Oh, isn't that cute. You have a picture of him signing trick-or-treat. Boy, I wish you would have told me Brynley was planning to take him. Tara was looking for a group of kids to go with Maddie."

"I didn't know," I admit as my voice fills with choked emotion. "You know, I stopped taking him trick-or-treating when he stopped talking and became uncomfortable around other people. I figured he wouldn't like it. I didn't want it to be awkward when he couldn't ask for candy. Brynley looked past all those concerns and took him anyway. Look at him! He is perfect."

"I know what you mean. If I had my way, I would protect Maddie from every bump, bruise, and scrape. I probably would lock her in a castle like Rapunzel to keep her from getting hurt. It's Tara that pushes me to think outside the box and push Maddie. It's funny, had you asked me before our daughter came into our lives about which one of us would be the most adventurous parent, I would've told you without a doubt it would be me. I was so wrong!"

"Brynley is making me second-guess every decision I've made about Brody. It upset me so much, I asked Brynley to leave. I had to grovel to ask her to come back when I realized I made a horrific mistake."

"If she's not supportive of you, why did you ask her to come back?" Aidan asks with a befuddled expression.

"Oh no, it's not that. It's just that for years it's only

been Brody and me. I am afraid of handling his issues incorrectly and causing more damage. We don't know what caused him to stop talking, so I'm not sure anyone knows what to do to encourage him to talk. So, I traveled all the way to Seattle to talk to a language specialist. He spent about ten minutes examining Brody before pronouncing that Brody was just choosing not to talk."

"Okay, so did he see any of Brody's testing or talk to his teachers or babysitters?"

"At the time, I assumed he did. But, now I just don't know."

Aidan winces. "That's rough. I have had all kinds of medical treatments over the years — some good and some bad. So, what changed?"

"Brynley came charging into our lives like a knight in shining armor. She didn't know about my therapeutic approach with Brody, so she just started signing. Brody has picked it up lightning-fast like he was just waiting for someone to give him a way to interact with the world. I feel so guilty! I could have been introducing some tools a long time ago if I hadn't listened to that blowhard specialist."

"Don't beat yourself up. Disability is tough, regardless of what kind you have. When I went to get my cochlear implants, there were as many experts telling me that it was a really bad idea and that it was going to ruin my life as I knew it. I was told that if I got implants, I would be selling out the whole deaf community for nothing because there was no guarantee my brain could even process the information from them."

"How did your parents even begin to make that kind of judgment call? Getting the implants destroyed your residual hearing, right?"

Aidan laughs wryly. "By that time, my parents had decided I was too much of a bother and they had ducked out of the picture. The decision fell to my guardian, Dolores. When we were facing a tough decision about whether to go ahead with surgery for Maddie, I asked Dolores how she made the decision to go ahead with the implants. You know what she told me? She said she had to disregard what the experts said and go with her heart and what she felt would increase my quality of living. I'm so glad she made that decision because it gave me back my music. I would be lost without it."

"Part of me can't help but wonder how far I've set Brody back by not introducing sign language earlier."

"You can't do that to yourself, Joe. You made the best decision you could with the information you had. When Brynley showed you a different way that worked better, you immediately changed course to help Brody. I know it's hard to accept, but kids are resilient. Think about Maddie, she spent most of her life in and out of hospitals and was clingy and withdrawn when she came to us. Now, she's a total chatterbox and fiercely independent."

"Yeah, she's really come out of her shell. I hope introducing sign language will help Brody do the same."

"We're going to stop for a meal break in a couple of exits. Why don't you make a video call home? I know that always makes me feel better when I miss my family."

"It's funny you should say that. Before Brynley came along, Brody and I had a pretty functional household. But since she's arrived, it finally feels like a real family."

"That's the way it's supposed to feel, buddy. Welcome to being in love."

I take a sip of my chocolate milkshake from the diner before I call Brynley on my iPad.

When Brynley answers, she has a glob of bubbles on her face and she is laughing. "Sorry it took me so long to get to the phone. Brody and I are doing the dishes and things got a little wild."

"I can see that. But why is Brody there with you? I thought he was with Mrs. Northrup."

"Umm … about that, I know you like Mrs. Northrup and all, but I'm not sure her home is the best place for Brody right now."

My brain starts to run a million miles an hour as I consider what Brynley's words might indicate. "What do you mean? Is Brody being hurt there?"

Brynley takes a paper towel and wipes her face before she says, "Oh, I'm sorry. I didn't mean to scare you. It's nothing as drastic as that. Brody tells me he's bored at her house and she isn't very supportive of our new communication plan."

I breathe a sigh. "Okay, I agree Mrs. Northrup's home might not be the most stimulating environment for him, but it's not like I have a ton of options."

"This isn't a long-term solution, but I worked out something so I have Brody covered till you come back from your tour."

"What do you mean? I thought you have to work."

Brynley tosses her hair over her shoulder as she lifts Brody up into her lap. "Well, I don't know if you know this, but it's grant season at Locate My Heart. It involves collating copious amounts of information and turning it into readable reports. Kendall told me I could come into the office in the morning and work from home in the afternoon. She says she has to get used to me working fewer hours anyway once my new job with the county starts. She says this will force her to get used to having me around less — without making her go cold turkey."

"Kendall is awesome, but what does that mean for us?"

"If you'd like me to, I can take Brody to school before I go to work and pick him up when his day is done. Then, we can come back to your house and I can work while Brody plays or watches movies."

In the corner of the screen, I see Brody nodding emphatically. "What do you say, Brody?"

What he says to me needs no interpretation. It's clear he is signing, "Want Brynley."

I look up at Brynley. "Well, that's clear enough. Are you sure you don't have a problem with this?"

"I think it's a great plan. I miss you and Brody so much when you're not around. Even when I was at work, I was thinking about how Brody was doing. Now, I'll know."

"Have you thought about how distracting it will be to have Brody underfoot? It's hard to think when his movies are blaring in the background. I would know, I try to write lyrics with him around and it's no use."

Brynley pats Brody on the thigh. "Go show your dad our solution to that problem."

Brody hops off of Brynley's lap and runs off-screen. "What was that all about?"

"You'll see. I think it's a splendid solution to our problem."

Brody runs back into the frame. This time, he's wearing a set of headphones that look like he's wearing a turtle on each side of his head. "Headphones? That's the solution to Brody's movies?"

"Oh, but these are not just any headphones. These are wireless Bluetooth headphones. We've already tested them with the television. Brody loves having his own personal sound system."

"You're a genius! I don't know why I didn't think about that."

"There are some lessons you don't forget when you grow up in a big extended family. Private space is at a premium, and sometimes you have to make your own. I can't tell you how many headsets and Walkmans I've been through in my life."

Brody taps Brynley on the arm and signs something about family.

Brynley's eyes mist. "That's a good question, Brody. I'm not sure where my family is."

Brody's next question is plain. I don't even need Brynley to interpret it for me. He uses Brynley's name sign and then asks her if she's sad.

Even through the limitations of video, I can see Brynley struggling to answer Brody's question.

"Yeah, buddy, I miss my family a bunch and it makes me sad."

Brody points at the phone screen and then to himself and Brynley. Then he makes the sign for family again.

"Thank you, Brody, I'm glad you and your dad are my family now. You guys make me happy!"

Brody grins at Brynley's expression and the silly sign for happy.

He looks up at her and signs something I don't

understand.

"Yes, you may go play. But say goodbye to your dad first."

Brody looks into the camera and blows me a kiss and waves goodbye. Then, I see him flash a sign I've seen my boss at the recording studio use thousands of times over the years at Silent Beats. My son, for the first time ever, just told me he loves me.

It is my undoing. I have to look away and wipe my eyes on my sleeve before I respond, "I love you too, Brody. I'll be home soon, I promise."

Brynley puts her arm around Brody. "Great job. You can go play now."

I wait a few moments for him to leave the room. "That was the first time he's ever told me he loves me. But, you knew that, right? I wish I would have been there to give him a hug. Still, it was sweet for you to teach him that."

Brynley shoots me a tearful grin. "I've got news for you, Daddy. I taught him how to say I love dinosaurs. All the rest of that is him. Every night before I tuck him in, I sign that I love him and that I hope he has good dreams. He changed the words to include you."

"Really? When he was a baby, I remember teaching him to say mama over and over again. I was hoping that would be his first word to Kara-Jane."

Brynley raises an eyebrow. "I take it that's not what happened?"

"At the time, I was sad — but in retrospect, it makes me very happy that Brody's first word was 'dada, dada, dada!' You should've seen the expression on my wife's face."

"I suspect she wasn't very pleased," Brynley guesses.

"That was one of many things Brody did to annoy her. So, she wasn't a big fan."

"Aww, that's sad. In the speech pathology class I took in college, I was taught that most babies have an easier time saying dada. It's just a developmental thing. She shouldn't have held it against him."

"So, you're saying it was nothing special?" I tease.

Brynley chuckles. "I said nothing of the sort. I'm sure Brody was quite intentional when he said your name first. Even if he wasn't back then, today was all about you."

My heart melts a little. "You're right. Today was epically special. I just wish I would've been there to celebrate with you guys in person. Sometimes, it sucks to be a working parent. I hate missing important things like this."

"I know. But I'm sure it's the first of many. If I catch him making the I love you sign, I'll try to get a picture of it so you can have it forever."

I clear my throat as a wave of emotion overtakes me. "Thanks, I would love that. You know, Brody isn't the only one I miss. There's a million things I want to talk to you about every day. I want to tell you what happened on stage and backstage and with my friends. I feel lost without you here. I don't know when or how we connected so deeply, but this is the first time I've ever missed anyone except Brody so much."

"I feel the same Joe Summers. Save those stories for me. You'll be home soon. In the meantime, I'll give Brody an extra kiss tonight when I tuck him into bed."

"You're a better woman than I deserve," I reply. "I'm not sure I'll ever find a way to pay you back."

"Don't be silly. No payback is necessary. This is a gift from my heart."

CHAPTER FOURTEEN

BRYNLEY

I CHECK MY APPEARANCE in the hallway mirror before we head out the door. "I don't know about this. Mariam is one smart cookie. She's going to figure out something is going on. I don't usually wear my hair in a fancy updo when I'm wearing jeans and a flannel shirt. Did I remember to put my dress shoes in the car with my dress? I'm still not sure how this quick-change operation is going to work. Where are we five women going to change our clothes?"

Joe puts his arm around my waist and pulls me close as he kisses my temple. "Relax! If there's anything this group does well, it's unusual weddings. I'm sure they got everything figured out. Jeff thinks like a military strategist and Tyler is actually a military strategist. They've done this dozens of times now."

I take a deep breath and let it out. "They have, haven't they? I'm kind of surprised Will and Kendall's mom and dad haven't had some sort of ceremony to honor their rekindled love."

"Oh, you didn't hear? Denny told me they renewed

their vows at a classic auto show in Vegas. Jennie apparently was in seventh heaven because they used an Elvis impersonator."

"That's funny! Norman deserves it, though. Kendall tells me he has worked really hard to stay clean and sober."

"Knowing Will, this will be an over-the-top wedding, the likes of which we've never seen before. So, buckle up and enjoy the ride."

Brody pulls on my belt loop. "Eat now?" he signs.

Joe chuckles. "Buddy, I'm gonna have to check you for a hollow leg. Didn't you just have a snack?"

Brody nods as he points to the pies in the box Joe just picked up and signs, "Want apple."

I reach out and ruffle Brody's hair. "I'm sure you do. I feel the same way. They smelled wonderful when we cooked them, didn't they? But we have to eat some healthy stuff first."

Brody's bottom lip pops out and he emphatically signs, "No!"

"All right, you say that now. But you haven't tasted Gwendolyn's cornbread stuffing and Denny's brined turkey. I think once you do, you'll change your mind."

Brody pulls out the book of vocabulary words I purchased him. He pages through carefully until he finds green beans. He points to the picture and signs, "Eat no!"

I sign as I speak, "There will be plenty of food there. You don't have to eat green beans unless you want to. Green bean casserole is actually really good. I think you should try it, just to make sure you don't like them."

Brody shakes his head no.

"That's too bad. But it just means more for Brynley

and me," Joe says as he sets the pies down to grab his car keys. He hands them to me. "Why don't you drive? I'll hold onto the pies."

"Oh good, I'll have something to focus on other than my nerves."

"I have faith that you will be amazing as always. This is supposed to be a fun day."

<hr>

As soon as we enter the Sawdust & Horseshoes lobby, it quickly becomes apparent why Aidan rented out a whole bar and restaurant. We're not even late and the whole place is packed.

Mindy stops us at the front door. "Hey, I like your hair. That'll save Aunt Donda some time. You brought your fancy clothes, right?"

"Of course! I had Joe check the car three times to make sure I had everything."

Mindy turns to Joe. "Go around the back of the building and knock on the red door. I'll let you in and show you where to put your clothes."

"Mindy, do you think she's figured it out yet?" I ask as I glance around the packed lobby.

"Not so far. Elijah is running interference and trying to keep her busy as people come in and out. She is getting a little annoyed with her little brother's persistent presence. When I was delivering my mom's fruit salad to the buffet line, I heard Mariam ask my husband why there are so many people here."

I grin and cover my mouth with my hand. "Oh, we are so busted — "

"I don't think so — at least not yet. When Justice

Gardner shows up, that might be a different story."

"Oh, that's a tough one. When he's in the room, there's usually a wedding to follow," Joe remarks with a smirk.

"Denny has a cover story. Isobel, Gracie and William are here because their oven broke at home."

Brody frowns.

Mindy notices and squats down to talk to Brody. "Don't worry, it's not really broken. William and his family are here to surprise my sister-in-law, Mariam."

Joe taps Mindy on the shoulder. "Would you mind signing? We are trying to teach Brody."

Mindy grins. "I can do that!" she signs. "I don't know if you remember me, but I'm M-I-N-D-Y," she finger spells.

Brody nods and signs song and points at Joe.

"You're right! I did sing a Christmas song with your dad. Have you heard it?"

Brody freezes and clutches my jean-clad leg.

Joe reaches out to pat Brody's shoulder. "Yeah, he's probably heard it hundreds of times. I played it a lot when we were trying to figure out the acoustic bridge."

Just then, we hear someone tapping on a glass and the chatter in the lobby ceases.

I hear Jerome bellow, "Who has something to be thankful for this year? I know I do because the Bossman says it's time to eat. You all better beat me to the buffet line, or I'll clean it out first. This is some fine-looking food."

Aidan chimes in, "Seriously, folks, eat up. If you don't, my wife is going to insist on bringing home leftovers and I'll have to let out my costumes. My wardrobe person would be totally ticked off."

Joe elbows me before he whispers in my ear, "I don't know about you, but I have much to be thankful for this year."

Thanks to my boots, I don't even have to stand on my tiptoes to brush a kiss across his cheek. "Me too. You'll never know how thankful I am that the store ran out of strawberry yogurt. That one oversight changed the course of my entire life."

Joe smiles at me tenderly. "I've been thinking about that a lot. I believe that if we hadn't met that night, we were fated to meet at another time. After all, our friends travel in the same circles. It's a weird coincidence that we never met before."

"Maybe the timing wasn't right."

Joe runs his fingertip down my jaw. "Our timing might not have been right before, but it's perfect now."

From behind me, I hear a voice ask, "Is that my best friend making googly eyes at a tall, handsome rock star?"

I laugh. "Yeah, the local billionaire inventor only wanted to be friends, so I found somebody else to date."

"Mariam has a bit of a crush on your guy, so I'm just grateful she chose me over the guitar player. It's not very often the nerds triumph over musicians. I'm counting my blessings."

"Very funny, Will," Joe says as he shakes my friend's hand. "You might be surprised at my nerdy tendencies. Even so, I'm grateful you passed on Brynley."

"Hey guys!" I protest. "It's not like I'm rotten produce at the grocery store or something."

Joe drops a light kiss on my lips. "I'm not saying that, Bryn. I'm just glad fate had someone else in mind for Will. I am thrilled beyond belief you are mine."

"Are these guys talking like cavemen again?" Mariam asks as she walks up behind Will and puts her arms around his waist.

I smirk at her characterization of the conversation. "Little bit. As a fiercely independent woman, I probably should object more than I do. It feels good to have someone claim me as their own."

"Oh, I know what you're saying, Brynley," Mariam says as she gives Will a squeeze. "Fortunately, I am happier than I've ever been, so it doesn't bother me."

Will turns around and kisses Mariam before turning back toward me. Will studies me carefully. "Whatever you guys are doing, you're doing it right. Happy looks amazing on you, Brynley. You have always been positive and optimistic, but you have an air of contentment I've never seen from you before."

Brody has had enough of our conversation and sets his Game Boy on the floor before he signs, "Eat now?"

Mariam laughs. "That's an excellent idea. Actually, that's what I came to tell you guys. If you don't hurry up, all of Kiera's mashed potatoes will be gone. You don't want to miss those."

"You sign?" I ask.

Mariam shrugs. "Most of us around here do. My brother, Elijah, learned in school and I picked it up from him. I've also been teaching art classes at Aidan's day camp for students with challenges. Many of them are deaf. So, it didn't take me long to learn a few basic signs. Some of them are less wholesome than others and I'm not as good as Tara by any means, but I get along."

"We are trying to teach Brody sign language since it's difficult for him to talk."

"Excellent, that's how my brother learned. His

Tourette's syndrome made him shy and reluctant to talk when he was young. Sign language provided a bridge."

I can't help myself, I flash a beaming smile at Joe. Despite his tic, Elijah can be quite chatty if he feels comfortable around you.

Joe leans over to whisper in my ear, "Maybe that's a good omen."

"That would be great, wouldn't it?" I whisper as I tuck Brody's Game Boy in my purse and grab his hand.

As soon as we enter the restaurant and join the line for the buffet, Brody starts examining the table. I can see he's getting agitated because he is rocking up onto his tiptoes.

"What's wrong?" I ask.

"Apple pie gone?" Brody signs with a questioning expression.

"Oh no, it's still there. Your daddy put it in the back with the other desserts. After everyone eats dinner, we'll have dessert."

"No green beans!" Brody signs stubbornly.

I look at the mountain of food on the long buffet table. "I don't think you have to worry. There's lots of other things to eat here."

Brody nods and signs, "Good!" with more than just a little sass.

I start stacking the dishes on the table. "I tried, but I couldn't even get him to take a single bite of green beans. Does that mean I am a complete failure in the mom role?" I ask as I watch Brody play with Kiera's son, Charlie.

"Nah, if that were true, parents everywhere would be dismal failures – me included. It's funny, Brody doesn't like green beans, but he loves broccoli. Go figure!"

"I was the same way as a kid. I couldn't stand tomato sauce in spaghetti, but I love pizza."

I glance over at the kids when I hear Brody let out a peal of laughter. My eyes widen when I see Charlie signing about the car chase he and Brody are conducting on the dance floor with matchbox cars.

"Charlie? Where did you learn to sign?"

He shrugs. "My sister, Becca, wants to be an interpreter when she grows up — just like Aunt Tara. So, she's been teaching me. It's cool, I can talk in class with my friend, Seth. The teacher doesn't even know!"

"Oh, I see. Did you know Brody is just learning to use sign language?"

Charlie nods. "Uncle Aidan told me, and I taught Brody how to say race car. Isn't that cool?"

"It's very cool. Thank you for helping," Joe says.

"We're going to race our cars down the hallway, is that okay?"

"That should be okay. Just make sure you don't run your cars into people," Joe instructs.

"Okay," Brody signs as he looks up at Joe before he scoops up the cars he was playing with and runs after Charlie.

Joe looks at me with tears in his eyes. "It's such a small thing. But it gets me every time. Thank you so much for teaching Brody sign language. I'm still stunned every time I get an answer from him. After so many years of silence, I never thought I would see the day."

I pick up his hand and kiss his knuckles. "It's the

least I could do. Families should be able to communicate with each other."

"Until Brody went silent, I never realized how magical communication truly is."

A piercing whistle goes through the restaurant and Will jumps up on the stage. "What are you doing?" Mariam asks with a slightly horrified expression on her face. "You're not going to make me get up there and sing, are you?"

Will shoots her a mischievous glance. "No ... not this time, but that would be fun, wouldn't it?"

"No! Absolutely not! That's Aidan's and Mindy's job," she protests as she hides her face.

"So, Mariam, love of my life ... remember when you said you would marry me any time and any place?"

"It seemed romantic at the time," Mariam quips. "Something tells me my words are about to come back to haunt me."

"Oh, I hope not. Because today is that time and that place," Will replies as he jumps off the stage and walks over to give Mariam a hug.

She sidesteps the hug. "Am I going to love you or hate you for this?"

"You're going to love it, I promise. We are going to make this the most special day you've ever had. I just didn't want you to get so stressed out about planning your wedding that you were too sick to enjoy it."

"I hope you did a good job planning it without me, William Benjamin Kordes! Forever is a long time for me to be mad at you. You better not be pulling a fast one on me."

"I wouldn't do that!" Will protests.

In unison, I and most of the audience present for his little announcement say, "Oh yes, you would!"

Will looks chagrined. "Okay, maybe in the old days, I would have. I'm in love now."

Mariam just shakes her head. "I hope I'm still in love with you by the time this crazy day is over."

Aidan jumps up on stage. "If you could all mingle on the dance floor, my crew needs to prepare for a wedding."

When Joe and I stand up to move, Brody comes running. "What?" he signs as he anxiously glances around.

I squat down and sign as I speak. "My friend Will is getting married because he is in love."

I blush when Brody asks me, "You and Dad marry?"

"Maybe someday," I stammer. "But right now, your dad and I are helping in my friend's wedding. It's his turn. So, we have to go change our clothes so we won't be late. Do you want to go with your dad or stay and play with Charlie and Becca?"

Without hesitation, Brody signs his answer. "Stay."

Joe ruffles his hair. "Okay, but be good. Make sure you take turns."

Brody nods and then signs a quick goodbye.

As we're walking to the dressing rooms in a back room of the restaurant, Joe taps Becca on the shoulder. "Hey Becca, do you mind if Brody hangs out with you guys for a while?"

Becca turns around and grins at Joe. "I'd be happy to watch him. I love kids — especially ones who sign like Uncle Aidan."

Joe chuckles. "I don't think Brody is quite there yet. He just started learning."

"That's okay. Anyone who hangs around us for very long tends to pick up sign language. It's kind of a thing with us."

"Yeah, I noticed. I guess if I had to move all the way across the nation, I landed in the right spot to help Brody."

"That's kind of a thing with us too. We help each other. So, don't worry about it. I'll keep an eye on him during the wedding."

I smile at Becca. "Thank you so much. Now, we have to go get beautified."

"You're going to have so much fun. My Aunt Donda is like a professional makeup artist."

My stomach flutters with nerves. "Wow! I can't believe this is really happening. I don't even want to think about how Mariam feels."

Joe puts his arm around my waist as we walk down the hall. "You want to tell me what my son asked you that made you turn red as a beet?"

I blow out a breath before I answer, "Brody wanted to know if you and I were going to get married."

Joe chuckles. "Maybe someday, but not today. Will would get a little bent out of shape. What did you tell Brody?"

"Pretty much the same thing. Are we scary, or what?"

"I don't know. I like being on the same wavelength as you," Joe leans over and kisses my temple. "I'll see you at the back of the aisle."

CHAPTER FIFTEEN

JOE

I TRY NOT TO fidget as Will fixes my cufflinks. "What am I doing here? I'm not a cufflink kind of guy. Give me flannel shirts and boots and I'm happy." With my other hand, I run my finger under my collar in an attempt to loosen it.

Jameson strains against his dress shirt. "You're not the only one. There's a reason the dress code is casual at Identity Bank West."

Will smirks at us. "Oh, quit your griping!" He points to me and remarks, "You're here because you are my best friend's main squeeze." He points at Jameson. "You're here because you're my brother-in-law and my sister knows how important this is to me. So, buck up buttercups. We're going to go out there and make our ladies drool."

"My lady drools even when I'm wearing sweatpants," Jameson teases.

Will comically covers his ears. "Oh shut up! I did not need to hear that about my sister — like ever."

"Seriously, Will, how is Mariam? Is the surprise

going to trigger a fibromyalgia flare?" I ask.

Will gives me a double-take. "I didn't know you were aware of her triggers."

"Wow! I know I play background acoustics, but I didn't realize I'm invisible. I played at the last fibromyalgia fundraiser Mariam organized."

"Sorry, Joe. That was a rough night. Mariam was in so much pain, I don't remember much else."

"So, she's feeling okay now?" I press.

"Yeah, so far so good. Her new regimen and the laser treatments seem to be helping."

Jameson nods. "It must feel amazing to be the inventor of a device to treat the pain of fibromyalgia. Kendall tells me the FDA approval process is moving right along."

"It is. They want another double-blind study. So, it could take a bit, but they don't seem opposed to approving our device," Will replies with a smile.

Elijah looks up from tying his shoe. Without warning, his hand comes up and strikes the side of his face. His Tourette's seems to be causing lots of tics today. "Jigger, jig, jig, my sister is so lucky to have found you. Knights in shining armor come in many different, jigger, jig, jig shapes and sizes. When you first told my sister you were going to help take her pain away, I had my doubts. But the device you invented seems to be working."

Elijah's hand flies up toward his face again. Will grimaces. "I haven't come up with a device to help you, but I'm still working on it. Those punches look painful. It would be great if I could invent devices to help both you and your sister."

Elijah rubs his jaw. "Jigger, jig, jig, if anyone can invent something like that, it's probably you. Speaking of my sister, we better go before she gets too anxious, jigger, jig, jig."

Will grins. "Let's go get me married. Heaven knows I've been waiting a long time. But, Mariam is worth it."

***

I know it's not my wedding, but when I take my place to walk down the aisle next to Brynley, she takes my breath away. Her hair is swept up and artfully curled and she is wearing a stunning red lace dress. When a child runs past and nearly knocks Brynley over, I place my hand on her back to steady her. It's then I discover her dress is open to the waist in the back.

"Nice," I murmur under my breath.

"You don't look so bad yourself," she whispers.

"You ready for this?" I ask softly.

"I never am — but somehow the weddings go on. This is not really my thing. I'd much rather hide behind the scenes."

"Maybe so. However, in my opinion, you are so amazing you should always be front and center."

From behind us, I hear a ruckus as someone comes to the door and sets her purse on a nearby chair. "Sorry I am late. Most people get married in a church! I wasn't looking for a cowboy bar."

Mariam pivots abruptly, which is difficult in her svelte lace dress and long train. She gasps when she sees her employee. "Izzy, what are you doing here?"

Denny hands Izzy a basket of flowers and petals. Isadora grins. "I'm your flower girl, silly."

Mariam raises an eyebrow. "Flower girl? Shouldn't you be a bridesmaid?"

"Will asked me what role I wanted to play in your wedding. I was totally honored to be included in your wedding since I work for you guys and everything. Anyway, I've never been a flower girl and I've always wanted to be. So, Will said that would be cool."

Mariam chuckles. "Far be it from me to stand between you and your dream. Please proceed."

Denny nods toward the stage. Usually, this is where I would be playing the wedding march. I'm surprised when I see Aidan and Elijah playing a soft instrumental piece I haven't heard before. It must be something Mindy wrote.

Brynley looks up at me with misty eyes. "Isn't that sweet, Elijah is playing guitar for his sister."

Isadora skips to the head of the line and starts throwing petals down the makeshift aisle. When she reaches the front, she turns around and beams at the audience. I've run into her several times at different charity events hosted by Will's company, Hallway Innovations, and I don't think I've ever seen her smile so big.

The audience starts to chuckle and I can't figure out what's going on for a minute. Then, I see Maddie and Charlie walking down the aisle. Maddie pushes her wheelchair for a few paces and then pauses as Charlie uses a kid-sized broom and dustpan to sweep up all the flower petals. They go a few more feet and repeat the process. They position themselves beside Izzy and turn to face the audience.

Like any proud mom, Tara is snapping a million pictures of Maddie.

Howard, the official wedding photographer, squats down beside her and says as he snaps a few shots with his large 35mm camera, "You can relax and enjoy yourself, Mrs. O'Brien. I got this one covered."

Mindy and Elijah are walking down the aisle when Charlie yells, "What's taking you so long? Maddie-n-me got here ages ago!"

The whole audience erupts in laughter. When Mindy and Elijah get up to the front, they place Charlie between them. Mindy blushes and addresses the audience. "I don't know if you could all tell, but Charlie is definitely my little brother through and through."

I glance at Brynley with a puzzled expression.

She tries to hide her grin as she explains, "I heard this story from Mindy's mom, Kiera. Apparently, during their wedding, Mindy did the same thing."

I'm used to seeing Kendall and Jameson in casual clothes. But I have to admit, they make a striking couple as they stride toward the front of the room. When Kendall gets there, Will hugs her and says, "Well, Sis, I'm finally doing this. Thanks for being such a good role model."

Will clears his throat and turns to his brother-in-law. "Hey, I need to apologize for razzing you at your wedding. I am a nervous wreck."

Jameson gives him a pat on the shoulder. "No worries. You'll do fine."

Mindy and Aidan transition to another song and Toby and Pauline practically waltz up the aisle. When they arrive, Toby shakes the groom's hand. Will's microphone picks up their whole conversation. "Couldn't happen to a nicer couple. Congratulations."

"I guess you guys are next," Will whispers without really whispering.

"Maybe, but you never know with this group,"

Pauline answers as she holds Toby's hand.

I place my hand on Brynley's arm. "We're up. You good?"

"I forgot to tell you I'm a big baby at weddings. I hope you have tissues." Brynley takes her fingers and wipes under her eyes. "Look at me, nothing has happened yet and I'm already a mess."

I pat my breast pocket. "I've got you covered."

"What if I start to ugly cry?" she whispers as we slowly make our way up the aisle.

"Even if you do, you'll always be beautiful to me."

As we walk by the next row of seats, Brody runs out and clings to my leg. Without missing a beat, Brynley picks him up and hitches him up on her hip and the three of us walk up the aisle.

When Will sees the unexpected development, he grins. "Heya, Brody. Why don't you go stand beside Maddie's wheelchair?" Brynley sets Brody down and he walks over to the kids. Everyone is watching intently, including Will, who instructs, "Try to hold still though. I'm a little nervous and I might get distracted."

Comically, Brody straightens his back and adopts a military posture.

"That's good, but you might want to breathe. Mariam told me nobody is allowed to pass out at our wedding."

Brody blows out his breath and then dramatically sucks in another breath.

"Close enough," Will quips as he watches Brody's antics. We are situated at an angle so we can watch both Mariam walk up the aisle with her lavish bouquet of red roses with a single white rose in the middle and Will's stunned reaction.

When Seth and Mariam get to the front, he carefully rearranges her veil to expose her face. Her father kisses her on the cheek and says, "My dear daughter, I could tell William was your *balibt* from the first time we met. I'm so glad you listened to your heart."

Mariam dabs at her eyes with a tissue. "You're right, Will is definitely my beloved. But I will always love you too, Daddy."

Justice Gardner steps up to the microphone. "Happy Thanksgiving, everyone. As the family and friends of Will and Mariam, we have much to be thankful for. Above all, we should be thankful that love grows in the most unlikely of circumstances. I have watched this young couple go through both triumphs and tough spots. Yet, their love prevails. The two of them have constructed their own vows. Honestly, this is a good thing because, like most of you, I have no idea what's going to happen next."

Mariam winks at Justice Gardner. "Judge, just take a deep breath and roll with the punches. That's my mantra for the day. I love my husband-to-be, but sometimes his creative nature scares the living daylights out of me. So, I'm going first so he can have a grand finale."

Mariam hands Kendall her bouquet before she pulls a little piece of paper from her bosom area.

She turns to the audience. "Sorry about this. It's going to be a little disjointed because *someone* forgot to tell me we were getting married today."

"Something tells me you'll do just fine, Mar. I've rarely seen you at a loss for words," Will responds as he grips her other hand.

"You should consider yourself lucky to be here today," Mariam begins.

A loud murmur erupts and travels through the crowd. Justice Gardner makes a motion to shush the crowd. "I'm sure it gets better." He turns to Mariam and asks, "It does, doesn't it?"

Mariam nods. "Infinitely."

The judge makes a motion for her to proceed.

Mariam clears her throat. "Anyway, as I was saying, you're lucky to be here because you made a terrible first impression. I thought you were a rich, snobby dude with absolutely no idea what it's like to struggle."

Will blushes and shrugs. "I didn't put my best foot forward, that's for sure."

"More than anyone, I should know better than to judge someone from outside appearances — but I made some terrible snap judgments about you."

"I probably deserved 'em," Will whispers, but his lapel microphone picks up every word.

"No, you didn't. You turned out to be the opposite of what I expected. You are kind and generous, even though people don't always extend that same kindness to you. You took my weaknesses and turned them into strengths. Most of all, you accepted me for who I am — with my flaws and everything. As if all that wasn't enough, you've made it your mission to use your skills to lessen the pain fibromyalgia causes in my life. For these reasons and a million others, I will love you forever, William Benjamin Kordes."

A collective sound of approval travels through the crowd.

A tear slides down Brynley's face and I hand her a tissue from my jacket pocket. She smiles gratefully and whispers, "True love is so beautiful."

William swallows hard and then takes a deep breath.

"I'm an expert at pretending. I've been doing it my whole life. My mask of rich, eccentric inventor hid a lot of shortcomings and insecurities. It turns out as I was pretending to be the kind of guy you deserve, you were helping me unearth the real William Kordes. You know, the ridiculously bright curious guy who struggles with everyday tasks like reading instructions or accounting reports. You encouraged me to ask for help and discover my true strengths without denying my struggles."

Will stops to cough and Elijah hands him a bottle of water. He takes a sip and hands it back.

"Mariam, you've given me the confidence to build my admittedly lucrative hobby to a thriving, well-respected business. Thanks to you, I now understand that all the money in the world doesn't buy happiness. Staying true to yourself, treating everyone with respect and love will earn you more happiness than you ever dreamed. Because I love you, I found a way to fall in love with my quirky self too."

"It's surprisingly easy to fall in love with you," Mariam admits as she pauses to hug Will.

Justice Gardner clears his throat. "Well, I guess we better get on with it. I understand you have rings to exchange."

Will nods. "We do, Your Honor."

Pauline hands him a small decorative pillow. Instead of the rings I saw when we were getting ready, these are paper rings made from gum wrappers.

Mariam and Will laugh out loud. "Officer Lawrence, I believe I may need to report a theft. I suspect my twin and her gargantuan husband," Will quips as he sticks his tongue out at Kendall.

Kendall raises an eyebrow. "Not that I'm admitting

anything, but you know what they say about paybacks —"

Maddie spins her wheelchair around, so she is facing Will. "Yeah, because of what you did at the last wedding, they wouldn't even trust me with the rings this time."

Mindy brushes the hair out of Maddie's face. "The ring thing at Kendall's wedding wasn't your fault. You weren't the ring bearer this time because we had a different job for you."

Justice Gardner holds out the gum wrapper rings. "Are we using these, or does someone else have the real ones?"

Brody starts to squirm and I place my hand on his shoulder to still him as I watch this latest snag with amused fascination. Brynley shoots me a small smile and rolls her eyes.

"They're real enough for now. We'll sort it out later," Mariam says with a shrug.

Justice Gardner's eyebrows climb toward his hairline. "Really? Are you sure?"

Mariam nods. "Rolling with the punches, remember? I have a feeling nothing is ever going to be typical in our marriage."

"All right then. Let's proceed." Justice Gardner hands each of them a gum wrapper ring.

Will smiles. "Whether it's a paper ring or 24 karat gold, this ring symbolizes the fact that our love has no beginning or end. We were meant for each other. I will love and support your hopes and dreams and love you in good times and bad."

Tears are streaming down Mariam's face and she has to stop to gently blot them away.

"These rings may be paper, but that doesn't diminish their meaning. I know without a shadow of a doubt you'll be with me in good times and bad. Heaven knows, bad times with me can be downright awful. Still, you are at my side cheering me on every step of the way. As your wife, with this ring — or any other ring — I promise to love you and support your hopes and dreams for all eternity."

Brody pulls on my pant leg. I glanced down at him and whisper, "Not right now, buddy. We're kind of busy."

Brody rolls his eyes. "I know!" he signs emphatically. He points to his pocket. I squat down and try to figure out what he needs. Much to my surprise, I find a little black velvet pouch. Brody grabs the pouch and runs over to Justice Gardner and stuffs it in his hand.

The judge peeks inside and grins. "Well, one mystery has been solved. Do we want to repeat the ring ceremony with the real thing?"

Mariam shakes her head. "No, I think the ring ceremony was more meaningful with these." She holds up her hand to show the audience. "To me, these rings are a reminder that even when you feel fragile and broken, love makes you strong."

"I couldn't have said it better myself. By the power vested in me by the state of Oregon, I pronounce you husband and wife."

Will gently holds Mariam in his arms as he announces, "It's about time! I have been wanting to do this since I ran into Mariam at Phoenix and Zoe's wedding." With that, he very thoroughly kisses his wife.

When they break off the kiss, Will looks a little dazed. "I have to say, it was worth the wait. Even better, I get to do that every day for the rest of my life. Isn't love grand?"

Chapter Sixteen

Brynley

I STARE UP AT the stage as Joe plays a beautifully complex bridge on his guitar. I am enthralled as the notes wash over me. Joe Summers is a stunning man any day of the week — but, he is downright compelling when all dressed up. I have to pinch myself every time I see him on stage. I am one lucky woman.

I feel someone tugging on my dress. I glance behind me, expecting it to be Brody, but it's Maddie. "You're supposed to be dancing. Why are you watching my daddy?"

"You're right, I said I would dance. But I was busy watching my friend Joe play his guitar."

"Joe is your boyfriend, huh?" Maddie asks as she looks back and forth between me and the stage.

I smile. "Yeah, I suppose he is."

"You probably should dance with your boyfriend instead of us."

I sigh wistfully. "I'd love to, but Joe and Aidan are a little busy right now."

"Be right back!" Maddie announces as she flies across the dance floor in her chair.

After she leaves, I notice Charlie is trying to teach Brody how to do the Macarena. I'm not sure I've ever seen the Macarena performed to a love song.

As the song winds down, a smattering of applause travels through the room. Aidan steps up to the mic. "Hey, Tasha and Jude!"

I glance over to the table where I last saw them and see them stop kissing and break apart as if they were just caught by the principal.

"If y'all aren't too busy being lovebirds, can you please come up and do a couple songs so I can dance with my wife and daughter? I had a special request and this is a wedding, after all."

Jude grins up at Aidan. "I'd love to, Boss — but I left my gear at home."

Aidan points off the stage toward three guitars on stands and quips, "Lucky for you, my wife always makes sure I'm over-prepared."

Tasha stands up and pulls Jude to his feet. "Come on, like Aidan said, it's only fair."

"*¡Eres tan mand!*" Jude mutters as he grabs his wife's hand and walks toward the stage.

Tasha stops in the middle of the dance floor and soundly kisses Jude. "I'm not even going to argue with you. I am bossy. But you wouldn't have me any other way."

"True enough, *Sirena*. Let's go make some music together."

Jude stops to grab a guitar before he and Tasha take center stage.

Joe gives Tasha a high five as he leaves the stage. I see him mouth the words, "I owe you one."

Tasha steps up to the microphone. A camera flash goes off beside me. At first, I am concerned because Aidan is trying to make sure this is a paparazzi-free zone. But then, I realize it's just Howard, Tasha's uncle. I mean, technically, he still works for a tabloid magazine. But, he is a sanctioned guest.

"Is everybody having a good time?" Tasha asks.

The crowd murmurs an affirmative response.

"I'd like to thank my number one fan, Hayden, for this song suggestion. Originally, *I Swear* was sung by John Michael Montgomery. This is our take on it. Jude and I think it's the perfect wedding song."

Joe strides over to me and takes my hand. "I've been waiting all day to ask you this. May I please have this dance."

I smile and brush a kiss across his lips. "I'd be honored." In the background, I hear a camera clicking and see a flash. Figuring Howard is just taking more pictures of his niece, I hold my hand out to Joe and we walk to the center of the dance floor.

He places his one hand on my waist and the other on my shoulder. He pulls me close and rests his chin on the top of my head. "I never thought I'd be this happy again. Thank you for making my life perfect," Joe murmurs as we start to dance.

At first, I'm overwhelmed by nerves. Silly dancing with the kids is one thing, but being held in Joe's arms is a whole other thing. I take a deep calming breath. I realize instantly I just made things harder on myself as I inhale the spicy scent of Joe's cologne. Without meaning to, I make a sound of appreciation.

Joe stops dancing for a second and looks down at me. "Is everything okay?"

I nod as I snuggle closer. "This is like a dream. It's been a long time since someone cherished me and held me close. It's so much better than just okay."

Joe leans over to kiss me lightly as we dance. Then, he murmurs against my temple, "I agree. This is pretty much my definition of happy."

I smile against his chest as I savor the feeling of being cocooned in his strong, sexy arms. I wish this day could go on forever. Yes, this is the stuff of fairytales. If I'm dreaming, I never want to wake up.

⸻ ◆ ⸻

I slap a stack of tabloids on the table at Panera's where my friends are gathered.

Kendall picks up the top one. "Nice picture."

"Yeah, that's the one Tasha's uncle took. It's actually a pretty nice story. The rest are much, much worse."

Tara grimaces. "I was hoping Joe would escape the downside of fame for a while. It's so tough on everyone. I mean to read the tabloids, you would think Jude and Tasha are on the verge of divorce every other week. I know that's not true. You should read some of the stuff they print about Aidan. He supposedly has love children in virtually every major city we've ever played in. Try not to take it personally, most of those tabloid reporters care very little about the actual facts."

Tasha takes a sip of her coffee. "Yeah. Trust me, Jude and I are just fine. The tabloids have no regard for the truth. I'm lucky Uncle Howard takes care of me as well as he does."

"I don't understand why your uncle would want to out Joe. I thought they were friends. Why would he do that to us?"

"We've been working with Howard for a long time. I suspect either he thought he was just sharing pictures from a friend's wedding or he had an idea that other tabloids were closing in with negative stories and wanted to counteract them. Howard doesn't usually run counter purposes to us," Tara observes.

"Obviously, Howard's efforts didn't do much." I show her one of the most vile, which announces, COUNTRY AND FOLK HEARTTHROB JOE SUMMERS FALLS FOR HOMELESS GRIFTER.

Jordan shakes her head when she sees it. "I swear, they have no sense of decency. Remember all that garbage they posted about Cristiano and me when Mishka went after me?"

"I know this isn't supposed to be personal, but to me, it feels like a slap in the face. Maybe it's because of my Roma heritage, but I don't like being equated to some thief who takes advantage of people. It sounds a little too much like Gypsy."

Madison comes around and gives me a hug. "I know it's hard not to feel like they're after you. It feels like a personal attack. But basically, all they're trying to do is sell papers."

"I'm trying to be optimistic, but this might spell the end of Joe and me. He is busy dealing with Brody. I can't add to his problems. That's not fair to either of them."

"The media attention that comes with stardom is rarely fair. But you can't let it change your relationship with Joe and Brody. He told Aidan that he finally feels like you're a family. Don't let a few jerks scare you away from that."

"I don't know. I can't shake my bad feeling. I always feared the other shoe would drop. I think this may be it."

Chapter Seventeen

Joe

I STRIDE INTO LOGAN'S office with my blood boiling. He looks up at me with a confused expression. "Is everything okay?"

I walk over to his desk and pick up his iPad. "You mind?"

"No, help yourself."

I pull up the websites Aidan showed me this morning and then hand the iPad to the head of security for Silent Beats.

He whistles softly through his teeth. "I didn't see these. I only saw the one that Howard put out there. That one wasn't so bad."

"Why is he putting anything out at all?" I seethe.

"Howard was probably trying to preemptively strike. He must've known what was coming."

"Oh, you mean like this?" I ask as I lean over his shoulder and click on another website. "That right there is a picture of my girlfriend taking my son to school. That is so far out of bounds, I can't even tell you!"

Logan scowls as he briefly scans the article and pictures put up by the rag magazine. "Yeah, I agree. Unfortunately, the more you protest, the more they cover you. If you antagonize them, pretty soon you won't even be able to fart without them reporting it."

"What am I supposed to do about this? I mean, Brody is starting to come out of his shell because of the sign language. He doesn't have meltdowns as often now. I don't want all of his progress to be erased because things are dangerous in the world around him."

"It might be a good idea to keep a lower profile. Maybe, they'll lose interest."

"No! I won't pretend I'm not seeing Brynley. She's the best thing that's ever happened to me. It's not just me either, you saw her at Will and Mariam's wedding. She is wonderful with Brody. You know what? I can have conversations with Brody now. I didn't make that happen. I tried for years to reach my child, but I couldn't. Brynley found what works. Not because I asked her to, but just because she tried to understand what was wrong with my son."

"I'm not suggesting the two of you split it permanently or anything. I'm just saying, a couple weeks apart might take the heat off."

"I can't believe you're suggesting that. Would you separate Katie from your son just because of media coverage?"

Logan spins his office chair around and stares at me. "Are you kidding me? Kadan would eat me alive. You remember the terrible twos, right? Katie is the only one who could make him happy."

"Exactly. So, you understand where I'm coming from."

"I got the impression you and Brody were doing just fine on your own before you met Brynley. I always admired that about you."

"Let's just say my definition of stable and happy has changed a bunch since Brynley arrived and I don't want that to disappear anytime soon."

"Understood. It was the same way with Katie and me. I thought I was fine on my own. I soon found out I'm a million times better with her by my side."

"So, how do we keep my girlfriend and son safe from these leeches?" I ask as I point to the iPad.

"Let me see if I can pull Howard and Aidan into this situation. Aidan has had more than his fair share of negative tabloid stories and Howard knows how the industry works. Maybe between us, we can come up with a workable plan."

"I hope so. For the first time in a long time, I look forward to getting up in the morning. I'm not ready to give that up."

"You shouldn't have to. We'll come up with something," Logan says as he writes himself a note. "By the way, being in love suits you," he says as I turn to leave the room.

***

Brody pulls on my sleeve as he practically runs into his classroom. There are alphabet charts and color displays everywhere. One wall is covered with children's artwork. He tugs on me until I follow him. "Which one is yours?" I voice my question as I awkwardly sign.

Brody's eyes sparkle mischievously. "Guess!" he signs, pointing to the wall of pictures.

I study each one carefully. "Oh, there it is. That's a very good picture of Scout and Brynley. Looks beautiful."

"Brody, I'm ready for you and your dad," Mrs. Appleton announces as she opens a thick folder.

Brody takes my hand and then motions for me to sit in one of the little plastic chairs in front of the teacher's table. I am a tall guy. This is not an easy feat. Brody takes one look at my knees, which are practically up by my ears and smirks as he settles comfortably into his seat.

"I'm glad you were able to come to this parent-teacher conference today, Mr. Summers. I understand you are pretty famous around here and tend to be gone on tour."

"I don't know if I'm all that famous and our band doesn't tour nearly as much as we used to before my boss adopted a daughter."

"That's good. Kids like Brody need a lot of stability in their lives."

"Kids like Brody?" I repeat blankly. "Don't all kids need stability?"

"You know what I mean," the teacher huffs.

"Actually, I don't. Is Brody having problems handling kindergarten? He always did well in preschool."

Mrs. Appleton leafs through a stack of papers. "Academically, your son is doing very well in class. He is one of our top students. Brody is bright, attentive and artistic. He seems to be much more engaged with the other students."

"Great!" I turn to Brody and sign, "Good job."

Brody smiles at me and signs, "Thanks."

The teacher clears her throat and continues, "As much as we are proud of Brody's accomplishments with sign language, his new abilities present a real problem in our classroom. Perhaps Brody would be better served in our contained classroom."

"Contained classroom? You mean you want to put him in special education? I thought you said he was excelling."

"He is. But now that he has started using sign language, it is more of a challenge to teach him effectively. He might fit in better with other children with disabilities."

My jaw drops open and I will myself to close it and calm down before I say, "You have to be kidding me! Brody can finally tell you what he wants and needs ... and now that's a bad thing?"

"Our regular teachers are not required to have training in sign language. So, he might be better served elsewhere."

"So, what you're telling me is my son is an exceptional student and you want to move him to a different environment because you are uncomfortable?" I ask incredulously.

"Using sign language is quite awkward and distracts from the learning environment for the other students."

"God forbid the other kids get to be bilingual because they learn sign language when they're young," I snap. "This meeting is over for now. I need some time to consider what you said."

"Like I said, Mr. Summers, I'm incredibly pleased with Brody's progress. We just need to find a solution that works for everyone."

———•◦•———

The kids are playing a raucous game of tag. I don't think I've ever heard Brody laugh so much.

Allegedly, I'm watching a NASCAR race with several members of the gang, but mostly we're just chilling. I'm told the women are having an informal meeting of the Girlfriend Posse. Who knows? With the way this group works, I could be getting married next and be the last person to know.

"Your little guy is doing much better. I used to think he was shy, but now I'm not so sure," Denny remarks as he watches the kids play.

"Yeah, he's come a long way. But his school seems to think that's a problem. I guess they liked him better when he couldn't talk back."

"Well, that's a bunch of burned soufflé!" Denny exclaims.

Burned soufflé. I turned the words over in my head a couple times before I realize it's one of the colloquialisms Denny uses instead of cussing.

"You're right. I think it's a bunch of BS. But I'm not sure what to do about it."

Aidan tunes into our conversation. "Wait! Are you telling me they are refusing to teach Brody?"

"Sort of. First, the teacher tells me Brody is a phenomenal student and performing well. Then, she tells me that it's too much work for the teacher, so they want to put him in a special contained classroom."

Aidan shakes his head in disbelief. "With all due respect, they're full of it. If he's doing well in his current environment, he needs to stay there."

"What do I do about the sign language thing?"

Aidan's friend, Tyler grins. "That's what people like Tara are for."

"You're saying I should get an interpreter for him? Brody isn't deaf. We had half a dozen different audiology exams with several doctors. They all agree he doesn't have a hearing problem."

"He doesn't really have to be to benefit from a sign language interpreter. It's clear from watching him play with Maddie and Charlie, knowing sign language has made it easier for him to connect with them. When Tara was in college, one of the students she worked with wasn't deaf at all but had processing issues. This student learned more from watching Tara sign than she did when people spoke to her. So, she used an interpreter to facilitate her learning style."

I look over at Jeff and ask, "You're the attorney, do you think I have the legal right to demand an interpreter instead of allowing Brody to be moved?"

Jeff nods. "Brody has the right to appropriate accommodations in the least restrictive setting. So, not only can you ask for an interpreter, I think you should."

Denny nods emphatically. "Don't you be letting them expect less of your son just because he's a little different. They used to do that all the time with Kiera. They'd take one look at her wheelchair and decide she was dumb as rocks. They couldn't have been more wrong about Kiera. So, don't be afraid to put up a stink to make sure Brody gets the best."

"Thanks. Brody amazes me every single day. I thank God for Brynley. Without her, Brody would still be locked away in his silent world. He's doing so well with the sign language, I'm going to press for him to have an interpreter. I may need to call you guys in for reinforcement because all this is new to me."

Tyler salutes me. "We may not have a cool name like the Girlfriend Posse, but we have your back. If you need something, just say the word."

<hr>

Aidan taps on the glass in the recording studio. He signs, "Need to take five."

I flash him the okay sign and take off my headphones. I pull my phone out of my pocket and scroll through my messages. I laugh when I see a meme from Brynley about the pitfalls of dating a musician. It's funny, but it's not wrong.

I just about jump off my stool when the phone rings. My eyes widen when I see who it's from. I cautiously answer, "Hello, Kara-Jane."

"Good grief, Joseph! You sound upset that I called," she huffs. "I thought you would be glad to hear from me. Don't you miss me?"

"Kara-Jane, it's been years since you've contacted me. You haven't even bothered to check on your son in all these years. So, I'm supposed to be overjoyed when you call me out of the blue?"

"Well … There's no need to be rude!"

"I was not rude. Rude is sleeping with my best friend and then abandoning your husband and child for years. That is the definition of rude."

"Okay, that's fair. I should've handled things differently. I'm sorry I hurt you, but I need to talk to you."

"You have me on the phone," I answer pointedly.

"I can't talk about this on the phone. Can you meet me somewhere?"

"You know I live in Oregon now, right? It's a long way from Florida and even further away from London."

"Yes, I know. I'm here now too. I can meet you at the food court in the Salem Center Mall. Please, Joseph, this is important. I wouldn't be calling if it wasn't."

"I'm at work right now. Let me see if I can take a long lunch. I'll call you back."

As I exit the recording studio, I snag Logan in the hall. "Would it be okay for me to take an extra hour for lunch? I've got to deal with some personal stuff."

"Everything okay with you and Brynley?" Logan asks with concern.

"Yeah, we're actually doing great. This has to do with my ex-wife."

"Kara-Jane?" Logan's eyebrows raise. "I thought she exited the picture a long time ago."

"She did. But, she just called and insisted on meeting me in person. She wouldn't discuss it on the phone."

"I wonder what she wants?"

I shrug. "Your guess is as good as mine. It's funny, I waited for years for her to call. Now that she has, I can't wait to get rid of her. Brynley has shown me what it's truly like to be loved. What I had with Kara-Jane pales in comparison."

"I hear you. I'll have Aidan do some paperwork. Heaven knows, he has plenty of it to keep him busy."

"I appreciate you running interference for me. Hopefully, this won't take long and I can get back into the studio. Things went pretty smoothly this morning."

"That's great to hear. With any luck, she's just being overly dramatic and you can get back to work soon."

"One can only hope. I'm going to take off so I can get this meeting behind me. I'll be back in a couple of hours."

As I unlock my car and throw my hat inside, my stomach turns. Whatever it is that brings Kara-Jane back in my life, it can't be good. Not only that, the timing absolutely sucks because Brynley and I are finally finding our footing again. Kara-Jane is a complication I don't need.

CHAPTER EIGHTEEN

BRYNLEY

WHEN I GET BACK from eating lunch at the local food truck, I see Kendall covering the receptionist's desk. Whoever is on the other end of the phone causes my boss to blanch white and sink down into an office chair. When she sees me, she jumps up, "Brynley, I think you need to take this in my office."

"Why would I need to take a call in your office? Everyone around here knows how to deal with confidential information."

"This isn't business, it's personal."

"Oh my gosh! Is something wrong with Brody?" I ask as I stand frozen in fear.

"I don't think so. Brace yourself, it sounds like a difficult situation."

I sprint toward Kendall's office with my heart beating in my throat. Given the nature of the horrific things we encounter at Locate My Heart, I can't imagine what Kendall's warning might mean. After all, we find missing children for a living and some of them don't come back alive.

The phone on Kendall's desk is ringing, so I breathlessly pick it up. "This is Brynley," I announce, trying to disguise my anxiety.

"Brynley, this is Logan. I need to let you know Joe has been involved in an accident. He is on his way to Sacred Heart Hospital."

My breath squeezes out of my mouth as if fate crushed my chest. "Oh no, what happened?"

"Details are sketchy right now. But somebody blew a stop sign and T-boned Joe. He's not being life-flighted, so that's a good thing. I think Rocco was the paramedic who scooped him up. Other than that, I don't know much."

"He got in an accident on the way to work?" I struggle to wrap my brain around Logan's words. "I don't understand. I was just texting with him about an hour ago. We were exchanging stupid memes."

"Joe stepped out for a long lunch. He said he had some personal business to attend to. He must not have made it."

"That's weird. He helped me make his sandwich for lunch this morning."

Logan clicks his tongue. "Brynley, focus. He's probably going to need you there with him. All this other stuff can be figured out later."

"You're right. My brain is going a million miles an hour." I glance up at the clock on Kendall's wall. "Oh crap! I have to go pick up Brody from school in a few minutes. I don't know what to do. Maybe I should call Mrs. Northrup."

"Becca is babysitting for Maddie. If you don't mind, you could probably bring Brody over here to play until we know what's going on. We've used her several times.

She is a very conscientious babysitter. Kadan loves her."

"Okay, that sounds better than any plan I have. I'll drop Brody by after I pick him up from kindergarten. Is Becca going to be okay if we have to stay late?"

"Yeah, she's really flexible. If she has to go home, Katie and I will watch Brody."

"I need to go compose myself before I freak out a little boy. See you in a few."

"Brynley, I've seen how you handle a crisis. You can do this," Logan advises.

"I know. Somehow, this feels entirely different. I won't breathe easy until I know Joe is okay."

"Me either. But Joe is tough. Don't give up hope yet — and a few prayers wouldn't hurt."

"Okay, gotta go." I hang up the phone abruptly. I feel like I'm moving in slow motion when the rest of the world is flying by at lightning speed. I have to pull myself together. Joe is going to be just fine. He has to be. We just figured it all out.

When I open the door to Kendall's office, she's standing on the other side with my coat and my purse.

As I pass my desk, I look at the stack of files and start to apologize and she puts her hand up. "Don't worry about it. Go figure out what's going on."

"Have I mentioned that you are the best boss ever?" I say as I rush out the door.

I hear Kendall yell at my back, "It's not hard to be a great boss when you have awesome employees. Don't worry about us. Just help Joe get better."

I rush into the emergency room and come face-to-face

with Rocco. As a paramedic, I figure he might know what happened. "Rocco! I'm so glad you're here. Do you know what happened? Logan couldn't tell me much."

"Some moron was driving while texting and plowed right into Joe. The good news is they weren't going as fast as they could have been, but there was still significant damage."

I swear, I want to throw up on the spot when I hear Rocco's assessment. He has been to thousands of emergencies in his career. If he thinks Joe's was serious, that's not a good sign.

"Damage to Joe or to Joe's car?" I press as I try to clarify what's going on.

"Raylene and I treated him on scene. His injuries are not immediately life-threatening, but scary nonetheless — especially when you consider who he is."

"What does that even mean?" I ask frantically.

Rocco puts his arm around my shoulder and walks me outside to a secluded seating area. "I can't say much because of patient confidentiality. Joe is likely going to be fine in terms of life and death, but his injuries could wreak havoc on his career. So, just be prepared."

I take a deep breath and blow it out. "Okay, thanks for the heads up."

"No problem. I hope he feels better soon. People who text and drive make me work twice as hard. Go on, he'll probably want to see you."

With shaky legs, I walk back toward the check-in desk and ask to see Joe Summers.

The lady at the desk scowls up at me. "You're not from the media, are you?"

"No! I do my best to protect Joe. You have no idea how awful some of those tabloids are. I'm Brynley

Meeker. I'm Joe's girlfriend." As if to underscore my point, I show her a picture of Brody, Joe, and me on my lock screen.

Unimpressed, the medical assistant studies the computer screen for a bit. Finally, she looks up at me. "Fine. Mr. Summers's personal security detail says you are on the approved list. Just ask for Mr. Summers once you've reached the nurses' station." She vaguely points down the hall.

I stand there for a moment, looking around, feeling very lost and small. From behind me, I hear Rocco say, "This way Brynley. I'll escort you back."

At the moment, I want to hug Rocco, but I'm afraid if I do, I'll completely fall apart. He places a gentle hand on my shoulder and guides me through the maze of hallways and medical equipment.

"Last I heard, Joe was in x-ray. I don't know if he's back yet. So, don't panic if he's not in the room."

"Okay, thanks for letting me know. It wouldn't take much to send my stress level through the roof."

When Rocco and I finally get to the ER, it's not difficult to tell which bay Joe is in. Josiah is guarding the door like the soldier he is.

Rocco nods at Josiah. "Here you go, Brynley. I hope things go well. I'm a big fan of Joe's."

Tentatively, I peek around the corner. I try not to gasp when I see Joe. It looks like he was in a boxing match and lost. His right eye is almost swollen shut and there is a goose egg on his head. However, my stomach drops to the floor when I see his left hand encased in bandages. I take a moment to compose myself before I walk over to the edge of his bed.

I stroke his thigh because his hand has an IV in it

and his other hand looks positively destroyed.

When he feels my touch, he struggles to open his eyes.

"Brody?" he whispers hoarsely.

"Taken care of. He is having an impromptu sleepover with Becca and Kadan. He was so busy playing from the moment he arrived, he barely looked up to tell me goodbye."

"Sorry," he says as he winces in pain.

"You don't have anything to be sorry for. Some thoughtless idiot hit you."

With his good hand he reaches up and rubs his goose egg. "Hurts. Was going somewhere important, but don't remember where." His IV machine starts to beep since he has his hand up in the air and is kinking the cord.

I fight to paste a smile on my face. "Looks like you're in for another long rest."

"Wasn't so bad last time," Joe mumbles. "Fell in love with you."

I squeeze his thigh gently. "Listen to you. You're even sweet when you're having a terrible day. I'm going to let you rest and see if I can get some information to make plans. The feeling is mutual, by the way."

"Okay," Joe's eyes drift shut. "I don't feel so good. I might really need help this time. Please don't leave."

"I'm not going anywhere. I just need to talk to some doctors. I'll be right back, I promise."

"Promise?" Joe asks.

"I give you my word," I vow.

I find Rocco sitting in a chair outside of the curtain.

When I see him, I ask, "You mind if we go somewhere and talk privately?"

"No problem. I know a quiet place we can go."

Rocco weaves me through the hallways until we come to a simple door. He opens it up and it's some sort of chapel.

"Oh, I don't want to disturb anyone else," I protest.

"It's all right. This isn't the main chapel. It's just a quiet prayer room. Most people don't even know it's here."

I sink down into one of the chairs after I grab a tissue from a nearby table.

"I need to make some plans," I announce abruptly.

"How can I help?" Rocco asks as I dab tears from my eyes.

"Is there any way we can get Jaxson to fix his hand? He's an orthopedic doctor, right? I've heard he is amazingly skilled."

"He is. I'll contact Dr. Shepherd – but I can almost guarantee you he'll want to call in a hand surgeon on this one. If I don't miss my guess, Joe has some crushed joints that will need to be rebuilt."

"Oh my gosh! His poor hand. Joe plays acoustic guitar for a living — he's going to be devastated."

"I know it's hard not to focus on the catastrophic effect of the accident, but aside from a heckuva concussion, the hand injury and broken arm seem to be his only serious injuries. If you could have seen his car, you would know how miraculous that outcome is. God had his hand on Joe's shoulder today. It could have been much, much worse."

"I need to figure out how to handle this with Brody.

He is going to be devastated when he sees his daddy hurt."

"I heard you tell Joe that Becca is babysitting Brody. How long can she continue to do that?"

"Becca told me not to worry about it because she's on winter break. So, a few days at least. I'll text her and ask her to keep Brody. Maybe she can go to the house and watch Scout too."

"Good idea. Becca sometimes pet sits for us. She's pretty flexible and the dogs love her."

I try to formulate some mental checklists and then I remember that Joe has more than one job. This accident is going to impact more than just his career as an acoustic guitar player. "Oh no! What about his teaching job? I know he only teaches part-time now, but he is going to need a substitute when winter break is over. I don't remember the name of his boss. He told me once in casual conversation, but I have no clue what he said." My hands tremble as I tuck my hair behind my ear.

"I'm sure if Logan doesn't already have that information on file, he can track it down. I'll send him a text message to remind him. Have you eaten lately?" Rocco asks me as my teeth start to chatter from the adrenaline dump.

I shrug. "I had some coffee this morning."

He reaches into his pocket and removes a protein bar and hands it to me. "These don't taste great, but you need to eat something. That's the thing about medicine. It's a hurry up and wait kind of deal. So, you need to keep up your strength because this is going to be a long haul."

My eyes widen as a thought occurs to me. "Oh my gosh! That nurse lady asked me if I was with the media. Do you suppose they've already figured out Joe is hurt?"

Rocco nods grimly. "Someone took a cell phone video at the scene and identified him. I'm pretty sure if they haven't already, the news stations and tabloids are going to pick it up quickly. Since his duet with Mindy, Joe has become a hot commodity. People know who he is."

I rub my temples. "Just what we need. Joe was hoping all the attention would die down after the wedding pictures were released. Is there anything I can do? The only thing I know about the media is that sometimes they're good for getting the word out about missing kids. I'm not sure how to protect Joe from all of this."

"I can't do anything about the tabloids, but I'm sure my wife, Mallory, would be more than happy to use her contacts with news organizations to be Joe's spokesperson with the media — unless you'd like another family member to do it."

"As far as I know, Joe doesn't have any family. Brody is it." I draw in a shaky breath. "This is all so daunting. I've never handled anything like this before."

"Look, you're doing fine. You have a workable plan. I'm going to contact Dr. Shepherd for you and you can send Becca a text. I'll contact Mallory and you guys can talk about the best way to handle the media."

"Okay, thank you so much." My mouth feels cotton-dry and my pulse is racing as I try to gather my thoughts.

"If you get overwhelmed, make sure to reach out to the Girlfriend Posse. I'm sure everyone will pitch in to help."

"Perfect. I'm not sure I'm ready to deal with everything by myself."

"That's what friends are for. Just say the word and you will have more help than you can handle."

"Thank you for keeping me calm today. You've been

a lifesaver." I reach out to squeeze his hand.

Rocco shrugs. "I'm glad to help. I learned a lot about medicine from the patient side of things when Mallory had breast cancer. I know it is scary and overwhelming."

I blow my nose on the tissue and stand up to throw it away. "Well, I better get back to Joe. He wants me to stay with him."

"That in itself is a very positive sign. Try to keep your chin up," Rocco says. "You need help finding your way back?"

"No, I've got it from here," I say as I place my purse strap over my shoulder and trudge back toward the ER. Before I enter, I take a deep breath to help counter the knot in my stomach. I've already lost one family that means the world to me and today I came precariously close to losing another.

Chapter Nineteen

Joe

My head feels like someone is trying to split it in two with an ax. I reach up to remove the offending weapon of torture and realize I have a needle stuck in the back of my hand. When I try to move my other hand, I can't. I start to breathe heavily. "What in the heck happened to me?" I mumble.

Someone stands up and moves closer to my bed. "Joe, try not to move so much. You've got wires and monitors everywhere."

"I can't move my arm," I practically screech.

"They used a temporary nerve block to help with your pain."

I struggle to sit up and examine my arm. "Holy Sh —" I start to say before a wave of pain overtakes me. "What happened to me?"

"You were hit by a car yesterday," Brynley answers.

I lean over and begin retching. Brynley quickly hands me a blue bag.

"Oh, your poor head," she murmurs. "The doctor

says you're nauseous because you have a concussion."

"What about my hand? What in the heck am I going to do about my hand?" I ask, my voice growing more strident with every word.

"Jaxson came in to look at it. He'd like you to see a hand surgeon. He's going to try to find one locally that he approves of. But he warned me that we might have to travel to Portland. You have a broken arm and you're in a temporary cast until your swelling goes down and they decide how to handle your hand injury."

As her words sink in, I reply, "I won't ever play the guitar again."

Brynley shakes her head. "Jaxson says they'll probably be able to repair the damage. It's just going to take some time and a lot of rehab. But you're not showing any signs of nerve damage. So, Jaxson seemed encouraged by that."

"How come I don't remember talking to Jaxson?" I mumble before I have to throw up again.

"Somebody tried to scramble your brain while it was still in your head. You have a pretty severe concussion. It's going to play tricks with your memory for a while."

I squint to focus my good eye and look around the room. "Where is Brody? I can't let him see me. I'll scare the crap out of him."

"Don't worry. Brody is with Becca. If the pictures she showed me of them playing with Play-Doh is any indication, he's having the time of his life."

I smile and that simple movement causes a bolt of pain to go through my face. "Thank you for taking care of everything. I would be even more of a mess without you."

Brynley reaches out and brushes some hair away

from my face. "Don't mention it. It's what I do for people I love."

<hr />

I have to stretch uncomfortably to reach the control for the television. I groan in pain after I grab the stupid thing. I vastly underestimated how bored I'd be in the hospital. Now, I feel bad for not spending more time with my dad before he passed away. Toward the end of his life, he spent a lot of time in the hospital. I tried to visit him, but until now, I didn't truly grasp how alone he must have felt.

After two days, I finally sent Brynley home to get some rest. She's been taking care of me around the clock. Don't get me wrong, the nursing staff has been wonderful, but sometimes it's awkward to contact them every time I need something.

I didn't expect the hospital to be quite so noisy. It's a different kind of noise than Brody generates. Unless he remembers to use his new wireless headphones, he always has something playing on the television. Sometimes, it's the annoying soundtracks of his video games. Often, it's both. Usually, this kind of background ambient noise drives me crazy, but I miss Brody something fierce and even his chaotic noise would be preferable to the cacophony of sound that echoes through the hospital hallways.

I click through the channels and smile when I run across a game show Brynley and I watched religiously a few months ago when I was so sick. I start to watch it before my pain medicine kicks in, and I drift off.

I wake up to the sounds of sobbing beside my bed. Alarmed, I struggle to find the buttons on the bed to sit it up. I look around the dim room to try to find the source of the sound. Oh my gosh! I hope Brynley didn't bring Brody by just yet. I'm sure I still look like a prizefighter who lost several rounds.

I jump when someone says, "Oh, thank goodness you're awake."

"Kara-Jane?" I ask when I recognize her voice. "What are you doing here?"

"Why shouldn't I be here? I'm your wife."

"No! You're not my wife. *Used* to be my wife and then you screwed my best friend and left. So, now you're my ex-wife."

"That's just a technicality. I never stopped caring about you."

"You're kidding, right?" I ask incredulously. "I literally haven't heard from you in years. Suddenly you're standing at the foot of my bed as if you have the right to be there. Why are you here, anyway? How did you even find out I was hurt?"

Kara-Jane blinks away tears. "Haven't you been watching the news? Your accident is a national news story. I was worried about you."

"That's rich! You haven't given a rat's butt about Brody and me over the past three years. You'll excuse me if I don't buy your line about being worried."

"Well, excuse me for caring. Besides, you agreed to see me, remember?"

"Why would I do something like that?"

"I don't know! Maybe because you're usually a nice guy, and I asked."

"Clearly, it must've been a lapse in judgment. I am too sick to deal with you. Please go away and let me get some rest."

"But, Joey, you're not up to taking care of yourself. You'll need someone like me around to help you."

I grit my teeth and it sends a shockwave of pain through my eye socket. "My name is Joe or Joseph. We are so far beyond nicknames. I have friends who are like family now. So, I am taken care of. Please, for the love of Pete, just go!"

As gingerly as I can, I lay the bed down and roll, so my back is facing her.

"You were never this rude before. I hope this is the pain medication talking and not who you are since you got famous."

"Goodbye, Kara-Jane. I'm supposed to be resting and you are not helping. I mean it. Go!"

CHAPTER TWENTY

BRYNLEY

I SET THE GROCERIES on the counter with a grunt. When Brody hears me, he runs into the kitchen and hugs my leg.

"Daddy home?" he signs as he looks around me to find Joe.

I squat down to his level and answer his question. "Not yet, Brody. Your daddy got hurt in a car accident. He has some broken bones and a big bump on his head. He has to stay in the hospital for a while. The doctor has to fix his owies before he can come home," I sign while I voice.

"Brynley help?" Brody asks with the innocence of a five-year-old.

I shake my head. "I'm pretty good if you have a tummy ache or a bad cold. But your daddy needs more help than I can give."

"Daddy hurt?" Brody signs.

"Yeah, he doesn't feel so good. The doctors are giving him medicine, so he doesn't hurt so much."

Brody rocks up onto the balls of his feet and signs, "I'm sad. Want Daddy."

"I know. I'll tell your dad how much you miss him. As soon as your dad is feeling better, I'll take you for a visit.

My eyes tear up when Brody signs, "Please today."

"I'm sorry, it probably won't be today … but soon, I promise. Are you having fun hanging out with Becca?"

His expression changes instantly as he signs, "Yes! Horses."

I look at him quizzically.

"I hope you don't mind, I took him to visit Uncle Tyler's horses because he got bored yesterday," Becca explains as she joins our conversation.

"Sounds perfect to me," I smile up at her. I turn back toward Brody. "Becca is going to hang out with you some more. I'm going to go visit your dad, so he's not all alone. Maybe you can do a video call with him later. I'll take your dad's phone charger with me. I bought your favorite kind of yogurt for breakfast. Be sure to share some with Becca. I bought extra. There is a surprise or two in those bags too." I point to the grocery sacks I brought in earlier.

Brody runs over to the counter, climbs on his stepstool and starts to unload the grocery bags I brought in.

I pull some money out of my pocket and try to discreetly hand it over to Becca.

She waves it off. "Don't worry about it. It's not as if you're just goofing off and going to dinner or something."

"Oh wow! You don't have to do that," I protest.

"I know. That's why it's fun. Besides, as a junior member of the Girlfriend Posse, I'm proud to help out my friends. Tell Joe I hope he feels better soon."

I briefly hug Becca. "You know you're about fifty billion kinds of awesome, right?"

Becca blushes. "If you say so. I'm just doing what needs to be done."

———— • ————

As I walk down the hospital corridor carrying two cups of hot chocolate, I notice there is a woman pacing in front of the door to Joe's room. I study her carefully to see if she is someone I recognize. Her blonde hair and cornflower blue eyes are memorable enough without even taking into account the large red rose tattooed on her neck. I'm positive I've never seen her before in my life.

Concerned she might be a nosy fan or a member of the paparazzi, I confront her. "Can I help you?"

She looks up and stops pacing. "No, I'm just waiting for my husband to wake up."

"Husband?" I repeat blankly as her identity becomes clear.

She glances at me as if I'm some sort of dolt. "Yes, my husband, Joe Summers."

Collecting myself, I set the hot chocolate on the charting counter near Joe's door and extend my hand for her to shake. "You must be, Kara-Jane, Joe's former wife. I'm Brynley."

Her eyes narrow and she ignores my extended hand. "Who exactly are you?"

"I'm Brynley Meeker, Joe's … friend."

Kara-Jane regards me as if I am dog poop she just scraped off the bottom of her shoe.

"'Friend', huh? It seems as if Joe's standards have slipped a little."

"Perhaps they have. Then again, they may have improved," I add pointedly.

"Rude much?" she snaps at me.

I shrug. "I was merely responding to your observation."

Kara-Jane picks up the cups of hot chocolate and heads toward Joe's door.

She makes a tilting move with her head. "You can go now. You're not needed here anymore. I'm his wife. If he needs someone to take care of him, I am available."

"That's nice, but I'm not sure Joe is available for you," I challenge.

She raises a haughty eyebrow. "I think he is. Did you know he was on his way to see me when the terrible tragedy happened?"

Her words cut me deeper than I care to admit. I attempt to play it cool and hide my pain. "Mmm-hmm, and how exactly did you learn Joe was injured?"

Kara-Jane rolls her eyes. "Are you dense? It's been all over the news."

"Well, I was contacted personally by people who love and support Joe. Maybe that difference should tell you something."

"I'm Joe's wife. He loved me first. He'll always love me best because I gave him Brody. Anything you get will just be leftovers."

I hitch my purse up on my shoulder and put my arms up in front of me in a hands-off motion. "You know what? I'll let the two of you sort it out. I don't need to be in the middle of this."

As I walk away, trying to preserve my dignity, one of my favorite nurses stops me several yards from Joe's room. "Are you okay? I know Joe was looking forward to your visit."

I look over my shoulder. "Apparently, he has a more important visitor today. If Joe asks, tell him I have Brody with me."

Brody is chilling out in the leather executive chair Jameson got her when Kendall was officially promoted to director at Locate My Heart. His headphones are on and he is playing a videogame. He is concentrating so hard on whatever he's doing, a tornado could touch down and I don't think he would notice.

I turn around and work on some last-minute paperwork. It's a good thing, it's near the holidays and things are quiet here. Fortunately, this is just stuff that needs to be finished and doesn't require a lot of brainpower. My mind is in many places today, but not much of it is focused on my job. I'm just trying to get through the day before I take a long bubble bath and have a good, long cry.

Even though I swore I wouldn't think about it, I can't seem to stop pondering the potential outcome. Tears are gathering in the corner of my eyes and I have to blow my nose. I jump when the chime over the door sounds. When I pivot toward the door, I smile through my tears when I see my friend, Will.

At first, he smiles back at me, but when he looks closer at my face, he scowls. "Oh no, you've been crying.

Please don't tell me your Prince Charming is doing worse."

"No, that's not it. Joe is doing much better. They were able to do hand surgery yesterday and put him in a solid cast. He has some titanium screws to hold everything together, but the hand surgeon is really hopeful that he will make a full recovery — even though it's his left hand. Joe is even able to keep food down now. The symptoms of his concussion seem to have abated and he isn't getting headaches as often."

Will walks over and gives me a hug. As he pulls away, he wipes away my remaining tears with his knuckle. "Color me confused. That all sounds like good news … so why the tears?"

"Because I was stupid. I let myself fall in love with a guy who is still tangled up with his ex. I swore I would never be the 'other woman'. Yet, here I am. I can't believe I fell for one of the oldest lines in the book."

"Wait, hold up! You're talking about Joe Summers here. He is as straight a shooter as they come. If Joe told you he was free to be with you, he is free as a bird! He would never deceive you. I saw you guys at my wedding and the other day at Joy and Tiers. I know when a guy is gone for a woman. Joe Summers is all in with you."

"So, why did Kara-Jane show up at the hospital?"

"I dunno. Money makes people do strange things. I'd know that better than anybody. Joe's music is climbing the charts. You know, they played at the Bluebird the last time they swung through Nashville. They don't feature you at the Bluebird unless you were at the top of your game. So, this ex of his probably caught wind of that and is trying to take advantage of him when he is down."

"Joe has been doing well for a while. She hasn't

contacted him in years. So, why now?" I lower my voice as I glance over at Brody. Thank goodness he is sound asleep with his headphones askew on his head as his body is slumped awkwardly in Kendall's office chair. "Poor Brody! I don't think he's been sleeping well without Joe around."

Will follows my gaze and chuckles softly. "That can't be comfortable. Is there still an old couch in the break room?"

I nod. "Gwendolyn crocheted us a cozy blanket. It should be on the back of the couch."

"If you want to get the door, I'll get little Mr. Sleepyhead."

Will gently lifts Brody up and cradles him against his chest. "Wow! He's really out. I miss those days," he whispers.

Will and I tuck the blanket around Brody on the couch and put some extra blankets on the floor in case he rolls over. Since he doesn't have his Bun-Bun, I grab a new stuffy from the supply I purchased to give to siblings of missing children and carefully place it next to him. He sighs and rolls over toward the back of the couch.

We pause to grab a coffee before we leave the break room. Back at Kendall's desk, Will picks up Brody's iPad and starts to scroll through the applications. "Didn't you tell me Brody is only five?"

I sit down at my desk and spin my chair around toward Will. "He's a little closer to six now. Why?"

"I own some of these apps. A few of these games are pretty advanced."

"Yeah, Brody is wicked smart. You should see how fast he's picking up sign language," I brag like a proud parent.

"Does he use this iPad a lot?"

I chuckle softly. "He carts that thing around almost as much as his stuffed bunny, Bun-Bun."

"You know, I could probably hook him up with something to help synthesize his speech. You know, like Stephen Hawking?"

I shake my head sadly. "That sounds amazing, Will. You might want to bring it up with Joe when he feels better because I am probably out of the picture."

"Do you want to be out of the picture?" Will asks as he studies me intently.

"Absolutely not. I don't want to leave — like ever. But I may not have a choice."

"You keep saying that, but what makes you think there's anything going on between Brody's mom and Joe? Last I heard, she had split and was long gone."

"I guess not. She said Joe was on his way to meet her when the accident happened."

"And you believe her?"

"Well … yeah. Logan told me that Joe left abruptly in the middle of the day to take a long lunch. It all fits."

"So, you haven't even spoken to Joe about this meeting and you've already assumed he's in love with his ex-wife based on a meeting which never occurred?" Will clutches his chest dramatically. "You know, I'm known for taking strange leaps in logic, but even I wouldn't decide my relationship is over before I even spoke to the person I love."

"But, Kara-Jane is correct. She'll always be Brody's mom and Joe's first love."

"Technically, she may be Brody's biological mother, but if she was a real mom who is in love with Joe, she would be in their lives. She's not there. You are. Don't let her buyer's remorse about her crappy lifestyle choices ruin your love and happiness."

I let out a strangled laugh. "Leave it to you to be blunt."

"I've learned some lessons in speaking my mind from my wife. If Mariam was here, she would tell you not to roll over and take this. Joe Summers loves you and his ex-wife is a virtual stranger at this point."

I close my eyes and shake my head to clear it. "*Argh!* I can't believe I let her psych me out. As usual, you are the smartest man I know. Wish me luck, I need to go tell my man that he is my heart wish and I am not going to step aside without a fight."

"Well, what are you waiting for?" Will demands.

I nod toward the break room. "Becca isn't here yet. I don't think Brody needs to be around for the showdown."

CHAPTER TWENTY-ONE

JOE

FROM MY COLD, STERILE hospital room, I look at my ex-wife as if she's grown two heads. "What did you just say?"

"No need to get all bent out of shape. I just told your plaything that she wasn't needed around here anymore because I'm here."

"Let me get this straight … You called me out of the blue and wouldn't give me a reason why you need to talk. Then, you took it upon yourself to dismiss the person I actually love just because you can't stand for me to be with someone else?"

"Umm, yeah! I read all about her in the tabloids. You're better off without her. You know that, right? She's bad news."

I shake my head and then regret my decision as a wave of dizziness hits. "The only bad news around here is you. Somewhere along the way, you seem to have conveniently forgotten you are my ex-wife. My concussion isn't so bad that I've forgotten our divorce. You don't have a right to say who leaves and who stays in my life. You gave up that right a long time ago!"

"Well, it's not that simple. You need someone to take care of you. I'm more qualified then whoever she is. I worked in a nursing home in Florida, remember?"

I stare at her as I try to contain my disgust. "My girlfriend's name is Brynley. You know better than to listen to the rag magazines. By the way, I do remember you used to work in a nursing home — as a dishwasher and busboy. With a Master's degree in social work, Brynley is eminently more qualified to take care of me than you are. You lost your chance years ago when you hooked up with Billy John."

Kara-Jane cringes. "Don't mention that jerk to me!"

"Trouble in paradise?" I ask sarcastically.

"Look, it's not my fault. Besides, you'd think that Billy would cut me some slack because I'm the mother of his children."

Even though I don't really want to know, curiosity gets the best of me. "What's not your fault?"

I swear, Kara-Jane's bottom lip slides out as if she's a toddler even though she's over thirty. I'm sure, I once found this behavior cute, but right now it's annoying the heck out of me.

"I'm pregnant, okay?" Kara-Jane huffs.

At some point in my life, this would have been devastating news for me. But now that I've discovered what true love means, I don't care what they do with their lives anymore. Pressing my lips into a thin line. I say, "Tell Billy John I said congratulations."

"You don't understand! The baby isn't Billy's. That's why he kicked me out."

I can't help myself, I laugh out loud and cringe when my ribs protest the unexpected motion. "Let me get this straight: You cheated on me with Billy John and left me alone to raise a child and then you cheated on Billy with someone else and left him with two children to raise?"

"You make me sound like an evil whore!" she exclaims with a horrified expression on her face.

"I'm just not sure who's going to raise this new one, that's all."

Kara-Jane's spine stiffens and her eyes are flashing with rage. "What do you mean? I'm a good mom. I love my kids!"

I set my jaw and stare at her silently.

She drops her gaze. "Well, I *want* to be a good mom. But it's really hard when you have to work as many hours as I do. I work my butt off for those kids and they still think Billy John walks on water. It is not fair."

White-hot rage courses through my body. I have to take several deep breaths before I can ask, "Have you ever once stopped to consider the fact that you are not the victim here? Your kids are."

"My girls are fine. It's just Billy who is being a jerk about all of this."

"Last I checked, you have three kids. You always seem to forget about our son."

"I'm not stupid. I didn't forget about Brody. There was just no point in fighting for him. I knew you'd never let me back into your life after what I did to you. So, why bother trying to have a relationship with a child I never see?"

Kara-Jane's attitude makes me livid. So, she doesn't deserve the whole story about Brody. I decide to give her just the highlights. "Not that you bothered to ask, or anything – but Brody is healthy, happy, funny, and full of energy. Not that I'm biased or anything, but Brody is flat-out adorable. I'm sorry you missed out on knowing a great human being."

"He's yours, not mine," Kara-Jane insists stubbornly.

"Brody is not something you can pick up and put down. No one owns him. Not you, not me, not Brynley — no one."

"Brynley this, and Brynley that," my ex-wife taunts snidely. "Do you know how sick I am of hearing her name?"

I lean back against my pillows and rub my temples. "If you don't like that I'm with Brynley, you can leave. No one asked you to be here. Which begs the question, why exactly are you here?"

Kara-Jane looks like I've punched her.

"I told you, I'm pregnant!"

"So? There's no question your child isn't mine, unless you've been pregnant for several years."

"What am I going to do? Billy John kicked me out, and I have no place to go."

"Gee, Kara-Jane, maybe you could get a job or spend some of my very generous alimony check on a place to live and getting medical care for your child."

"You owe me that money. You stole my child."

"What kind of drugs have you been taking? Last I checked, you and loverboy were cleaning our bank account out and headed out of town to live in another country. The only reason I knew what happened to you is because I happened to come home sick from work on the day you guys split. How exactly does that translate into me stealing your child?"

"That's what it felt like," she counters petulantly.

"Facts are facts, Kara-Jane. The fact is, you left

Brody and me without even a second glance. I waited years for you to come back, but now I've moved on."

A look of stark fear crossed with undisguised rage fills Kara-Jane's face. "What about me?"

"What about you? You're not my problem anymore. Go cry on someone else's shoulder."

Kara-Jane studies me shrewdly. "You're not in a position to fight back right now. You might want to think about that. I could do real damage to you. After all, I was in here while you were asleep. I'm sure the tabloids would be interested in the story of how I tried to rescue my son from you since you're so grievously injured you can't take care of him, but in a drug-fueled craze, you refused to let me see my son."

"Are you serious? It's hard to believe we ever loved each other. You're willing to try to destroy me and Brody because I won't support a child who isn't mine?"

She shrugs. "A girl's gotta do what a girl has to do. It would be cheaper in the long run for you just to help me, but the choice is yours."

"For me, the choice is simple. I choose Brody… and Brynley. Do your best. My friends who know us know what really happened. I've had enough of you. Do I need to call my bodyguard to escort you out of the hospital?"

Kara-Jane's eyes about pop out of her head. "You have your own personal bodyguard?"

"I do. Unlike you, I don't use my kid as an excuse not to work hard and be successful. I gotta tell you, I know why you thought I'd be willing to help you, but you're barking up the wrong tree. Goodbye Kara-Jane."

Brynley isn't answering her phone. Crap! She must've believed all the garbage Kara-Jane was spewing at her."

After a couple hours, I send Will Kordes a message. "I know Brynley is your best friend. Can you do me a favor and let her know that my ex-wife is full of hot air and venom. I don't know how Kara-Jane threatened Brynley, but I'm almost positive she did. Whatever Kara-Jane said, it's not true. Maybe Brynley will listen to you."

As soon as I send that text message, my phone rings. I pick it up. "Go for Joe."

"Duuuuuuddde!' Will replies. "I don't know what kind of twisted sociopath you have for an ex, but she sure did a number on Brynley."

"What do you mean?" I ask with a feeling of dread in the pit of my stomach. Maybe Kara-Jane has already started her campaign against Brynley.

"I don't know exactly what was said word for word, but whatever it was, it convinced Brynley that you're still in love with your ex-wife. In fact, the way Brynley tells it maybe she isn't even your ex."

"Oh my gosh! How in the world does Kara-Jane come up with garbage like that? She left me! She also signed the divorce papers giving me full custody of Brody and the judge terminated her parental rights. I absolutely don't love Kara-Jane. Even if I was in love with Kara-Jane once upon a time, my love dissipated when she left and didn't come back for Brody. Right now, what I feel for her borders a little more on hate."

"It's often that way with our exes," Will answers philosophically.

"No, you don't understand. She's been gone for

years and didn't even ask about Brody. She gave birth to the child. How could she completely ignore him? The only reason she was interested in him is because she wants to use him as a weapon against Brynley and me. She wants to prove I'm not able to take care of Brody because I'm injured."

"Oh, good luck with that! One call to the Girlfriend Posse and her case would be totally destroyed. I can see why you don't like her."

"Honestly, I don't know her all that well anymore. Who knows what she's capable of doing?"

"All I have to say is bring it on. You're an amazing father. If she tries to prove otherwise, she'll be sorry out of luck."

"She seems bent on destroying Brynley too. We've been divorced for years. Now that I'm finally with somebody I love, she suddenly wants to make a claim on me? I'm not okay with that."

"Okay, we need a plan. The first part of the plan is to get Brynley back on your side. She's feeling kind of lost right now. I think there is a part of her that fears what Kara-Jane told her is true. You need to show her it's not."

"I'm gonna need your help because Brynley won't return my emails, phone calls or texts."

Will groans. "I love Brynley to pieces, but when that woman has made up her mind about something, it's almost impossible to get her to listen. I'll do my best."

CHAPTER TWENTY-TWO

BRYNLEY

I BUNDLE UP IN a scarf to disguise the fact that my face is red and blotchy. I thought I had reached peak sadness when my family disowned me. I was wrong. Losing Joe has practically destroyed me.

I walk into Joy and Tiers to get my hot chocolate and pastry. Instead of a smile, Heather has a pensive, tense expression. That's okay, it matches my mood. So, I pay for my food and sit in the little waiting area for it to be ready. Heather shakes her head. "Don't sit there."

"What?" I asked, startled by her instructions. "I always sit here."

"Umm, today you can't. They need to be … cleaned. Go sit over in the bridal consulting area. I'll bring you your food. I'm a little backed up today, so it'll be a couple of minutes."

"Oh, okay," I answer, confused by her weird request and demeanor. I guess I may not be the only person having an off day.

I head toward the corner of the store. Two huge murals frame the area Heather uses for wedding cakes.

The pictures depicting Tara and Aidan and Heather and Tyler's love stories are too much for me to take. So, I sit and watch people hustle down the street in the frigid rain.

I'm lost in thought when I hear Heather clear her throat. When I look up, Heather has my hot chocolate and blueberry scone. I was expecting that. What I wasn't expecting was the huge group of people standing around her. These are all my adopted community that I consider family.

"What are you guys doing here?" I ask Will and Kendall.

"We're staging an intervention," my boss answers.

"I don't understand. What are you talking about? I don't drink or take drugs."

"Rumor has it you're fighting with your fella again," Denny explains.

I sigh as a tear rolls down my cheek. "Denny, I wish it was that simple. I would give anything for it to be just a simple disagreement. But it's not. Joe belongs to somebody else and my heart is shattered."

Mindy steps forward and puts a hand on my shoulder. "I've been Joe's singing partner for a long time — even when he was still living in Florida. He may have loved his wife at one time, but he loves you now. Trust me when I tell you there's nothing between them. But you and Joe need to figure this out as soon as possible so you can protect your family."

"I don't have any family. They disowned me. Joe doesn't have any either," I point out.

"There are lots of ways to define who your family is. You and Joe need to be on the same page — like yesterday."

"What about Kara-Jane?" I blurt.

"You know how Mindy said your family can appear in many different ways?" Tara answers. "The same is true of your enemies. They aren't always who you think they are."

"I know how you and Mindy's predictions work. Are you trying to tell me Kara-Jane was out-and-out lying to me?"

Madison steps forward. "Look, I don't have any psychic gifts like these guys, but as someone whose spouse had a psychotic ex-wife, I'm telling you flat out that she was lying. Don't let her destroy your relationship. She has absolutely no claim on your boyfriend."

Kendall nods. "I'm not telling you how to live your life, Brynley. I spent too many years trying to be someone I wasn't just to make someone happy. All I'm saying is that if you love Joe, you might want to consider making a claim of your own."

"What are you guys suggesting? Do you think I should ask Joe to marry me or something?"

Rocco holds up Mallory's hand as it's intertwined with his. "It's not unheard of in this group. If that's how you feel, I say go for it."

Mallory grins. "You never know, Joe may think it's the most romantic thing ever."

"You guys are sure Kara-Jane is full of it?" I question.

Gwendolyn steps toward the front of the group. "I know you don't know me very well, but I have had first-hand experience dealing with narcissistic bullies. I can tell you without a doubt, that woman has no current relationship with Joe. It's debatable whether she had much of a relationship with him in the past, either, but that's a topic for another day. Joe made it clear to us months ago that he was head over heels in love with you. That hasn't changed. If anything, the difficulties you have been facing have brought you closer together."

I glance down at my phone, which shows repeated calls and messages from Joe.

"I suppose I better swallow my pride and let Joe know how I really feel."

My group of friends applauds my announcement. "You all are crazy, you know that? Who else receives relationship advice when ambushed by a flash mob?"

Heather shrugs. "Honestly, we've done weirder stuff. Go pick out some goodies from the case to take to Joe. He's probably sick of hospital food."

Kendall walks over and hugs my shoulders. "Don't bother to come in today. Your heart wish is waiting for you and you guys have a future to figure out."

"Okay, okay, I'm going. You guys are way pushy and I love you for it."

"Young lady, I expect an update after you have sorted your life. We care about you guys and want you to be happy."

"I know. That's what makes my pretend family way cooler than my actual family."

Will puts his arm around my waist as we walk toward the pastry displays. "My sister-in-law said some interesting things. You might want to pay attention. As far as I know, Mindy has never been wrong."

My stomach lurches. "I'll watch my back," I promise.

———◆———

I drop a bag of Joe's favorite pastries on the bedside table.

The movement wakes him up. "Hey, I hear you're looking for me." I walk over and drop a kiss on his cheek.

Initially, Joe looks startled to see me. However, he quickly recovers. "I'm glad to see you, but why have you been avoiding me for days? I've tried calling, sending text messages ... and even emails, but I got no response from you."

"You seemed busy," I mumble as I study the tile floor.

"You mean Kara-Jane?"

"Of course, I mean her. You don't have any other exes who might make random appearances in your life, do you?"

"No!" Joe rakes his hand through his messy hair. "Look, I didn't invite the one who showed up. Last I saw her, she was headed to conquer the United Kingdom with a guy I used to consider my best friend."

I raise an eyebrow. "Funny, that's not what she says."

"Kara-Jane also says she's a good mom." Joe shifts position in bed and moans. "My former wife is a tad delusional."

"She said you agreed to meet with her before your accident — "

"If I did — and that's a mighty big if because I don't remember — it was because I wanted her to understand what she threw away."

I sit down on the edge of his bed. "So, you never planned to go back to her so that Brody has his real mom?"

"Heck no! Kara-Jane never cared much for being a mother. She cared less about being a good wife. Brody and I deserve better. She can take a flying leap for all I care. I don't even know how she tracked me down in

Oregon."

I shake my head. "You and Mindy have only had the most popular Christmas song for two years running. The radio stations start playing Silver Bells practically in August. You're kinda hard to miss."

Joe shrugs. "Yeah, I guess. I've had other hits and she didn't seem to care then."

I hesitate for a few seconds before I reply, "I have a theory."

"Please share because nothing Kara-Jane ever does makes any sense to me."

"Well, I don't know exactly when she resurfaced. But I have a hunch it's after all the tabloids covered Will and Mariam's wedding. The picture Howard shot of us while we were dancing pretty much says far more than a million words."

"People take pictures of me all the time. Why would this one be any different?"

"Since we started hanging out together, I've noticed the way you pose for selfies with fans. You are always very careful to keep a respectful distance. It was not hard to tell your body language was completely different with me."

"Why would Kara-Jane even care? She hasn't been around for the majority of Brody's life."

"I've worked around kids my whole life. You know what makes a toy you discarded much more attractive?"

"Another kid wanting to play with it?" Joe answers with a chuckle.

"Exactly! As long as no one else loved you, she felt free to ignore you, but as soon as someone mattered to you, she felt the need to pound on her chest and make a claim."

"Well, she has no claim on me. She should've stayed on the other side of the United States – or better yet on another continent."

"Aren't you worried about Brody resenting you for cutting his mom out of his life?"

"Not especially. She left without so much as a backward glance. I haven't purposefully kept Brody away from her, but she hasn't shown any interest in actually being a mother."

"I don't know what to say to that. I absolutely adore Brody. I can't imagine leaving his life now that I just came into it."

"Like I said, being a mother was not Kara-Jane's strong suit. There's a reason the judge gave me full custody."

I chew on my thumbnail nervously. "So, if she's not here to get to know Brody, why is she here? Is she trying to get you back or something? Doesn't she understand you and Brody are a package deal?"

"I assume she does. But she was here because she thought I would bail her out of her latest jam."

My jaw goes slack. "Really? After what she did to you? That takes some stones."

"You have no idea. It's more than just stones. Would you believe she popped back into my life because she's pregnant?"

"Pregnant?" I stammer as soon as I compose myself.

"Yeah, you believe it? Kara-Jane was stupid enough to cheat on me with my best friend, and now she is sleeping around on him."

"Well, that's gross. It's really tacky for her to drag you into her mess just because you're famous."

"You're preaching to the choir. But unfortunately, Kara-Jane believes that just because we were once real good friends that she can take a dump on me anytime she wants to. You know what's crazy?"

Mutely, I shake my head.

"Before I met you, I would have fallen for every single word of her sob story."

I give a startled burst of laughter. "So, what you're saying is being with me helps preserve your sanity?"

"I couldn't say it better myself," Joe says as he reaches out to grab my hand. "Please don't disappear again."

"I don't plan to. But things like this are going to come up again." I announce pessimistically.

"What is puzzling me is why you believed her? I thought I made it clear who I love. If you're not getting that message, I'm doing something completely wrong."

"Wrong?" I ask, feeling lost in the conversation.

"I make my living talking about love. Even so, maybe I haven't been clear enough about what's between us."

I stand up and start to pace at the foot of the bed. "This is kind of hard to explain. Kara-Jane managed to hit every button of insecurity I have. Family means so much to me because mine disowned me. I didn't want to be the one who stood in the way of you and Brody having a complete family."

"But *we* are a fam —" Joe starts to interrupt.

I hold up my hand to stop him. "I didn't say it was reasonable. I have all sorts of hang-ups when it comes to my family. I thought I'd put it all behind me, but I guess I haven't really. Life has taught me I can't trust people who say they love me. I can't count the number of times that my family and friends switched their loyalty to other people and left me twisting in the wind. I was sure you were going to toss me aside like almost every other person in my life has done. When Kara-Jane came back, I figured it would be easier for me to duck out of the picture first before you could hurt me. When I say it out loud, it sounds ridiculous, but I can't help the way I feel. I'm sorry I panicked."

"Regardless of what she says, Kara-Jane doesn't have any place in my life. The judge terminated her parental rights. Genetically, Kara-Jane may be his mother, but Brody is all mine. If I have anything to say about it, she won't have any contact with Brody. Ever. My love for her died a long time ago when she chose my best friend over Brody and me. I'm done with her today, tomorrow, and for infinity times infinity."

I clear my throat gently. "Maybe Kara-Jane doesn't understand that things have changed between you," I charitably offer.

"Oh, she understands the score. She changed her mind far, far too late and now she is livid about her choices."

I walk back over to Joe's bed and grasp his hand. "I understand how she feels. If you were mine and I let you go, I'd be a tad bit upset too."

Joe lifts my hand and kisses the back of it. "There is no 'if' involved. I *am* yours. Nothing Kara-Jane says or does is going to change that."

<hr>

I throw my purse on the booth at Joy and Tiers and slump down in my seat. I glance over at Kiera, who is currently my supervisor as I complete the last requirement for my

Master's degree in Social Work. "Is it always this hard? I don't know how you've done this for years."

Kiera shrugs. "Today was especially tough. Sometimes the kids don't feel comfortable telling us the real truth even when the evidence is staring us straight in the face."

"I know. I just wish I could have done more."

"We all feel that way. The moment days like today stop bothering you is the day you need to quit."

Heather leans forward to put the pitcher of iced tea back into the center of the table. "Tara, remember how it was when Kiera started? We used to have to make a Panera run every few days just to de-stress her."

Tara nods toward the corner where Maddie, Lydia, and Charlie are sitting at a table coloring. "Yeah, who knew back then how much our lives would change in just a few years."

Madison winks at me. "You might want to make an escape plan. I swear, there's something in the water around here. Everyone ends up pregnant."

Heather gasps. "How did you know? I haven't even told Tyler yet!"

Madison stares blankly at her sister for a moment. "Shut the front door! Really?"

Tara wilts in relief. "Oh, thank goodness you finally told us. This was a tough secret to keep from everyone. I wanted to spill the beans every other day."

Heather whirls around and faces Tara. "You knew? Why didn't you say anything? You could have saved me a very expensive trip to the ER."

"Not my place," Tara answers solemnly. "Your morning sickness wasn't really a matter of life and death."

"Could've fooled me," Heather mumbles. "I thought I was going to die."

Madison points at Kiera. "Trust me, we've been there, done that and survived. The good thing about pregnancy is it only lasts a few months."

Heather looks glum. "Tyler and I have waited so long for this to happen. I had just about given up. I thought I would be ecstatic. Instead, I'm just sick, tired, and grumpy. What if I'm not cut out for motherhood?"

Tara openly scoffs. "If there was ever a job you were born to do, it's being a mother. Look at me, if I can figure it out, so can you."

Kiera turns her gaze toward me. "How is motherhood treating you?"

"Me? I don't think I really count."

"If I'm the mother of this little jumping bean they tell me is a baby, then you can call yourself a mother," Heather insists.

"Did you, or did you not just nurse Brody through a wicked case of the stomach flu?" Madison asks.

"Well … yeah. It hit right after Joe got out of the hospital. It's not like he was in any shape to handle it."

Madison wrinkles her nose. "Trust me, dealing with the flail gives you honorary motherhood status."

I frown and stir my iced tea. "Unfortunately, Brody has a mom and it's not me. She's back in the picture and I'm not sure what that means for us."

Mindy looks up from the book she's reading and stares directly at me. "Joe already told you that. You need to believe him because soon, you'll have to rely on your love to get you through."

"What does that mean? I mean, Joe told me Kara-

Jane means nothing to him now. But how could that be? She's tall and glamorous. She's got more moxie in her little finger than I have in my whole body."

Heather smirks. "Uh-huh. She also apparently has the brainpower of a gnat because she was stupid enough to walk away from Joseph Summers."

"Well, there is that."

"Exactly! You're not that stupid, right?"

"No, I'm definitely not that dumb. But sometimes, it's hard to believe that this isn't all too good to be true. I'm scared to death."

"True love is a gamble and scary as heck, but it's worth it," Heather says as she bolts to her feet and runs toward the restroom. "Or at least I hope it's worth it."

"Oh my gosh! Why are you crying?" Kendall exclaims as she walks through the front door of Locate My Heart.

I pivot the computer monitor toward her. She can't miss the screaming headline. BITTER FIGHT WITH GYPSY CAUSES NEAR FATAL RESULTS FOR JOE SUMMERS!

Kendall cringes. "Ouch! I'm so sorry."

"Joe and Brody don't need this garbage. He needs to be focused on physical therapy instead of protecting me. I hope Brody doesn't see this."

"It's too bad Howard's attempts at misdirection didn't work. No disrespect to Howard, but I've developed a strong dislike for his whole occupation. I don't even want to know where they got their supposed 'inside scoop.'"

Heat rushes into my face as I try to keep my voice

even. "Oh, there is no question about that. See those pictures of Joe in the hospital? I didn't take those and I'm sure no one at Silent Beats took them either. The only other person besides hospital staff who has been admitted to Joe's room is Kara-Jane. She threatened to destroy Joe after he turned her down. I guess she figures destroying me is the easiest way to hurt him."

Kendall studies the computer a little more closely. "That is too low for words. I wonder how she got the picture of you and Brody?"

My stomach lurches. "That picture is from last week when I took Brody to the park. He is crying because he'd just fell off the merry-go-round and got a sliver. She had to be stalking me."

"Wow! Have you talked to Joe about this? What does he think?"

"Umm, I haven't really told him yet. He is staying away from his phone and computer because he is having a hard time not using his fingers on his dominant hand. I guess this has been out for a couple of days, I only know about it because somebody from my other job asked me if it was true."

Kendall's eyes widen. "You mean they actually had to ask you? Anyone who knows you knows you're the best thing that's ever happened to Joe Summers."

I shrug. "I'm new over there. You know, some people believe every word the tabloids write. My grandma did. She always thought she would run into Elvis at the grocery store."

"That's just crazy! I don't understand how they can just make stuff up, which is clearly not true. You wouldn't believe some of the stuff they've posted about the families of our missing kids. Still, I think you should probably give Joe a heads up so he can bump up his protection. If Kara-Jane is out to get him, maybe he needs to take legal action."

I sigh heavily. "I know you're right. I just hate to add one more thing to Joe's plate. He is so happy to be out of the hospital."

"You know this isn't your fault, right? It's one of the pitfalls of being famous. Jameson says sooner or later, it happens to anyone who is successful, whether they are in the entertainment industry or not."

The bell above the front door rings and I brace myself for an incoming case. It's only nine o'clock in the morning, but for some reason, it feels like it should be quitting time.

Kendall glances over at me. "You look exhausted. I'll get this one."

I nod as I mouth the words, "Thank you!" I put my earbuds in and grab the stack of files I've been working on. A few moments later, I look up and find Kendall walking toward my desk with an odd expression on her face.

My heart plummets toward my toes. "Oh no! How many this time?" I ask as I pull new file folders out of the drawer to set up new missing child cases.

"Thank goodness, that's not it. But you may want to head to the conference room. You may need some privacy for this."

Shakily, I make it to my feet. "Please tell me nothing happened to Joe or Brody," I plead in a hoarse whisper.

Kendall puts her hand on my shoulder. "This has nothing to do with Joe or Brody. Take a deep breath. It's gonna be fine."

"So, why are you sending me to the conference

room?" I ask with trepidation.

"Trust me, you'll appreciate the privacy. You can take the rest of the day off if you want to."

"Kendall, you're scaring me to death! Why would I need to take the day off? Is something horrible about to happen?"

She shakes her head emphatically. "No, I don't think so, or at least I hope not. Go!"

Reluctantly, I head toward the conference room. Just for safety I stop and grab a box of tissues off of the intern's desk.

Once I enter the conference room, I am too nervous to sit down. So, I pace up and down the side of the room. After what seems like forever, I hear a soft knock on the door frame. When I look up, my jaw drops open. "Lavina? Oh my gosh! You're so grown-up!"

"You look so old! What's with the glasses?" my sister asks as she runs into my arms.

I gather her in my arms and squeeze tightly for what seems like hours. The shell of pain around my heart that I keep hidden from everyone else cracks just a little.

"This is what happens when you get old and study too much. I had to get computer glasses. Thanks for noticing Squirt."

"It's a good thing you weren't wearing them in the picture I saw. If you had been, I would've had a harder time recognizing you."

I swallow hard. "Which picture?"

Lavina pulls away and sits on the edge of the conference table. "You know, one of those gossip magazines mom loves to get? We went to the grocery store yesterday and she threw it in the backseat. It just opened to your picture. I almost screamed when I saw it."

I audibly groan. "Please tell me mom didn't see that article —"

"Nope, the twins got into a fight and distracted her. I put it in my school notebook and took it to my room."

I slump down in a chair next to my little sister. "It would have broken her heart if she'd seen it. I bet it won't be a secret long. I know how gossip travels."

"You didn't really do all those things to Mr. Summers, did you? Mindy Whitaker is one of my favorite musicians and he plays guitar with her."

The corner of my mouth hitches up. "I know. Mindy and I are friends."

"No way! Are you serious? You like really know her?"

"I do. We went out for dinner the other day. To answer your other question: No, I didn't do any of those things that nasty article accused me of."

"Is it true Mr. Summers is married?"

I roll my eyes. "You really think I would steal somebody's man? It's true, Joe used to be married, but he's been divorced for a long time."

"You've been away from home for a long time. Maybe you changed —"

"I moved away to go to school. It didn't change who I am as a person." I pause as a thought occurs to me. "What did mom and dad tell you about why I left home?"

Lavina stares at the carpet for several seconds before she says, "Dad says you're an ungrateful snot who betrayed our family."

Her words pierce my heart. "Lavina, you just turned eighteen, right? Are you married yet?"

A horrified expression crosses Lavina's face. "No! I

can't even find a decent guy. Why would I get married?"

"Well, I didn't want to get married either. That's why there was a huge fight that split up our family. When I was still sixteen, Dad decided I needed to marry the son of the richest man in our community because he thought it would be good for business."

My sister's eyes widen and she wrinkles her nose. "They wanted you to marry Manfri? No disrespect or anything, but you're not his type."

"You think? Whatever clued you in?"

"Manfri is married now. His wife is really nice. But she is as quiet as a mouse. All she does is cook and clean all day."

"Okay, to be fair, these days I do a lot more cooking and cleaning than I used to. Quiet? Not so much."

"Did Mom and Dad think you were in love with Manfri?"

"No, they knew I wasn't. So, when I stood up to them and told them I didn't want to marry somebody I didn't love, they disowned me."

"Oh, that's sad. I thought you left because you didn't love us anymore."

I stand up and give her another hug. "Lavi, I've never stopped loving my family. I'll love you forever. I'm just not welcome in our parents' home."

"That's just stupid!"

"I know. But I couldn't marry somebody just to help make money. That's wrong. Besides, I had my own dreams."

Lavina frowns. "Yeah, I know all about that. Dad about blew a gasket when I told him I wanted to grow up to be a lawyer. He told me that all lawyers are shysters and that it's a boy's job."

"My friend Jeff is a lawyer. He tells me that many law schools have more female students than male. So, Dad is a little behind the times."

"Your friend isn't a thief, is he?"

"No, Jeff and my boss Kiera are definitely not thieves. They are the kindest people I know. You might be interested to know that they are Mindy's parents."

"I still can't believe you know these people."

"Okay, I know you didn't come here to hang out with my rich and famous friends. Why did you go to all this trouble to find me?"

Lavina glares at me. "Oh don't mind me, I'm just your baby sister. It's not like I missed you or anything."

"Sis, I've been gone for a while. Why now?"

"You were always so good at busting me. Honestly, I thought you moved far away since we haven't heard from you in forever. So, when I saw your name in the tabloid, I did some online research and found that picture of you when you got an award for your charity work. That's how I figured out where you work."

"Oh … I completely forgot about that. It was a couple years ago that I got an honor from the governor. At least it was a better picture than the one in the tabloid."

"Uh … I guess I'll just come out with it then. Mom and Dad want to move. They say we've been in one spot for too long. They keep rambling on about our ancestral roots and how we need to be faithful to them. I don't want to move to another state. I got accepted at Oregon State University. They have a pre-law program that would allow me to get my JD in six years. They even offered me a partial scholarship. I don't want to lose all that now."

"Congratulations! What do you need to make that happen?"

Lavina cringes. "A place to live until school starts next fall? I don't want to leave with them, but I have to show them I can make it on my own without them here."

"You can stay for a few days, but let me think about the long-term plans. My life is kind of a chaotic mess right now. If we do this, we have to tell them what's going on."

Lavina smiles mischievously. "Okay with me. I mean, what's the worst they could do, hate us?"

I sigh. "I know that doesn't seem so catastrophic to you — but I can tell you it's no fun. Hopefully, they've mellowed over the years."

"Don't hold your breath," Lavina mutters. Suddenly, her face brightens. "While I'm here, can I meet your friends?"

I chuckle. "You know, not all my friends are famous musicians."

Lavina grins. "Yeah, I know. Still, some of them are, and that's good enough for me."

Chapter Twenty-Three

Joe

I AM STRUGGLING TO get the lid off of a new container of orange juice. Until my hand and arm were mangled, I didn't really realize how much you need both hands to get by. Just as I'm about to let loose with a string of cuss words my mother would disown me for, Brynley comes through the back door with a pensive expression on her face.

"How many kids are missing this time?" I ask with a feeling of dread.

Brynley walks over to the counter and sets her purse down. She opens the orange juice, pours me a glass, and adds a few ice cubes. "You may want to sit down for this." She places her arm around my waist and walks with me as she carries my juice over to the couch.

"Oh man, it's babies this time, isn't it?"

"This time, it's more about who has been found – or rather who found me."

My befuddled expression prompts her to continue. "This is a long story and I need to start at the beginning."

I lean back against the couch cushion and cautiously

take a drink of my juice. I'm still not used to doing things with my right hand.

"Remember when you told me how bent out of shape Kara-Jane was when you told her you wouldn't help her?"

"Uh-huh, she threatened almost everything short of burning me alive."

Brynley hands me a tabloid folded back to reveal pictures of us. "Unfortunately, there is little doubt she adopted a scorched earth approach."

"Seriously? She took a picture of me in the hospital. I can't believe I once trusted her and thought I loved her."

"Brace yourself, it gets worse," Brynley cautions as she turns the page.

I gasp when I see the two-page spread featuring pictures of Brody mid-meltdown while Brynley is clearly trying to comfort him. When I read the caption under each picture, I feel a visceral sense of rage. "Are they crazy? You were not hurting Brody while I laid helpless in my hospital bed! You're the reason Brody wasn't traumatized any more than he was. I'm going to contact Jeff and see if we can sue for libel or something. They shouldn't be able to get away with this!"

"I agree with you, but there's a bigger issue here," Brynley replies softly.

"What bigger issue? Kara-Jane and whoever these creeps are who call themselves reporters have set out to completely destroy your reputation. You work with traumatized children, who knows what your supervisors are going to make of this filth?"

Brynley looks like I sucker-punched her. "I wasn't talking about that, but thank you for reminding me that this is so much worse than I first imagined."

I wince at the pain in her voice. "I'll just shut up now."

"Anyway, what I was trying to tell you is I didn't see anyone in the park taking pictures of us. I have no idea how they got those. You might want to contact Logan to see about upping your protection detail to include Brody."

"Consider it done. But I'm not going to stop at just Brody. You are equally precious to me. I will not let Kara-Jane destroy what we have."

Brynley lets out a shuttered breath as tears gather in the corners of her eyes. "Thank you, you have no idea what that means to me. But, there's something else too —"

"You mean it gets worse than this?" I ask as I gesture toward the tabloid magazine I threw on the coffee table.

Brynley gives me a ghost of a smile. "No, for a change, this is actually good news. Or, at least, I hope it is."

I breathe out a sigh of relief. "After the last few months, I would love to have some good news."

Brynley gestures at the coffee table, "So, as much as I hate this whole mess, this nightmare actually brought some good news into my life. My baby sister, Lavina, was able to find me because she saw the article."

I swing around and hug Brynley as well as I can with my arm in a cast. "Oh, Bryn! That's amazing. I know you miss your family something awful. Where is your sister now?"

Brynley blushes. "Sitting in my car."

"What? It's cold outside!"

"I wasn't sure what you would think of my family

just popping in — especially since you don't feel so well."

"Brynley, Brody — and now you — are the only family I have left. Of course, I want to meet your sister, your brothers, and your parents if they're around."

For the first time since Brynley came home, her smile goes all the way to her eyes as she says, "For now, it's just Lavina, but maybe that will change."

"Go get her. After we pick up Brody from Mrs. Northrup's house, we can all go out to pizza or something."

"Are you sure we should be seen in public after all the lies that were printed about us? Won't that damage your career?"

"Brynley, just stop. If we let Kara-Jane's ambush change the way we live our lives, then she wins. I wasn't ashamed of you last week, I'm not ashamed of our relationship now and I'll never be. You are the best thing that's ever happened to Brody and me. If the media can't handle that, then I'll just have to lose fans. I'm not gonna lose you because Kara-Jane decided to be a witch."

"Okay, I'll go get Lavina. Be forewarned, the two of us together can be a little much."

"I'm looking forward to the challenge," I reply as I lean over and kiss her lightly. "I can't wait to meet another Meeker."

⎯⎯⎯◆⎯⎯⎯

"So, you guys really met in a grocery store? That is so cool. It's like a whole romance novel!"

Lavina looks over at Brody as he is making the sign for soup. "What is he doing?"

"Brody is telling you that we went shopping for

chicken soup that night," I explain.

"Is he deaf or something?"

"Lavina! Rude much?" Brynley scolds.

I shake my head. "Brody has had several hearing tests. He definitely isn't deaf, but for some reason, he is unable to talk."

Brynley reaches out and touches my forearm. "That's not true anymore. Brody may not speak in the language everyone knows, but he can communicate very well."

"I talk," Brody signs. I automatically voice his words for Lavina. It's hard not to snicker when Brody signs, "You understand no," as he points at Brynley's sister.

At first, Lavina looks a little stunned. Then, she bursts out laughing. "You're right, I'm going to have to do some catching up. Maybe you can teach me?"

Brody nods and signs, "Okay."

I start to translate his sign and Lavina shakes her head. "I got that one." She repeats the sign a couple times and Brody grins from ear to ear. "That's so cool!"

Brynley ruffles Brody's hair. "Yeah, my buddy here is all kinds of cool!"

"Wow, you guys are like a little family. So, why does everybody hate you?"

Brynley's jaw sets. "Most people don't hate Joe. One person is on a vendetta to destroy his career."

I take a deep breath and blow it out. "Lavina, how old are you again?"

"I'm eighteen," she answers with a puzzled expression.

As I try to fish quarters out of my pocket with my right hand, I look up at Brynley. "Hey, this restaurant has some really cool video games. You want to go play with Brody?"

As I'm still trying to dig the change out of my pocket, Brynley grins and pulls out a roll of quarters from her purse. "Way ahead of you. Remember, this place has a vintage Pac-Man machine. Brody beat me last time, so I'm ready for a rematch."

Lavina glances back and forth between me and Brynley. "Um, should I go with her?"

I shake my head. "I need to talk to you for a second."

Brynley's sister settles back into her chair. "Oh, okay —"

I watched as Brody takes Brynley's hand and drags her toward the arcade corner in the pizza joint.

"Am I in trouble for something?" Lavina asks.

I clear my throat. "No, that's not it at all. I'm just about to be brutally honest with you and that is not a conversation my son needs to hear. Someday, perhaps. But, not today."

Lavina leans forward in her chair. "Oh boy! Does this mean I've been moved up to the grown-up table?"

I chuckle. "I suppose you have. Are you ready?"

She scoffs. "I've been ready since I was eleven. I've just been waiting for somebody to notice."

"I get it. So, just so you know, I love your sister in a way I never dreamed was possible."

"That's nice. Because it would really suck if she was hanging around and you were indifferent."

"Funny. If there's one thing I've never felt toward your sister, it's indifference. No one is more surprised than me."

"Way to dis Bryn!" she exclaims.

"What? Oh wait … I didn't mean that the way it sounded. You see, when I was barely older than you, I married my beautiful, vivacious high school sweetheart."

Lavina crosses her arms and glares at me.

"Let me finish the whole story before you judge. So, Kara-Jane and I got married when we were ridiculously young. She was my number one fan. I can't tell you how many times we had to sleep in the back of my van because I couldn't afford a hotel room where I was performing. It was okay, though, because we lived in Florida and were young enough to think it was still one big grand adventure."

"I bet Florida is warmer than Oregon."

"It is, but I don't miss the hurricanes. So, anyway … it soon became clear I wouldn't be able to support us on just my music gigs or my songwriting. So, when I turned twenty-one, I inherited money from my mom. I used that to go to college to become a teacher because I knew that's what my mother would've wanted me to do."

"I'm sorry your mom died."

"Thanks. So, everything was going along okay. I was still doing some gigs on the weekends while going to school. I even had a part-time job, so I thought things were okay. But then Kara-Jane got pregnant with Brody."

"So, I guess you must've missed your health class about what prevents that from happening."

I roll my eyes. "No, I know good and well what causes babies. It's just that the doctor told Kara-Jane that she would probably never be able to have any kids. After a while, we just took that for granted."

Lavina smirks. "Surprise!"

"You got it. Kara-Jane never wanted to settle down

and be a mom. I just didn't realize how much she would hate it. I thought it was just pregnancy hormones. Soon, I was juggling my job, my last year of college and a newborn."

"What was she doing?" Lavina asks incredulously.

"That's a really good question. I don't know how long it had been going on because I was completely oblivious, but my wife was sleeping with a guy I thought was my best friend. We played together in my band."

"Ouch!"

"Uh-huh. Even though I was devastated, I never thought she would leave. I'd been in love with her since I was fourteen. Up until a few weeks ago, the last view I had of my wife was her surrounded by suitcases playing tonsil hockey with Billy John."

"What happened a few weeks ago?"

"Well, you know what they say about karma? So, Billy John thought he scored big when Kara-Jane chose him. But, what goes around comes around and eventually, she left him too."

"It's hard to feel sorry for him because he stole your wife, but still, that's pretty scummy of her. So, was she trying to get you back?"

"I'm not exactly sure what her plan was. I think she thought that I would just welcome her with open arms even though she walked out of our lives and never looked back, even for Brody."

"I take it you kicked her to the curb?"

"Yeah! It's not my fault she was pregnant again with some random dude's child."

"I thought she said she couldn't have any kids?"

"Yeah, that was always my understanding.

Apparently, I was wrong because Brody has several half-siblings. Anyway, she wasn't happy with my decision and threatened to destroy the career she helped build."

"What about Brody? How could she walk away from him a second time?"

"I have no idea. She was so bent on my destruction, she never even bothered to meet him. However, given what she's done, I can't say I'm particularly sad their paths did not cross."

"I guess not. But what does this mean for my sister?"

"Between my accident and whatever shenanigans Kara-Jane is pulling, Brynley is pretty scared. I'll do everything I can to protect her from Kara-Jane's hate, but, honestly, I don't know how unhinged my former wife actually is."

"That's not what I want to hear. I want you to tell me everything is under control and that psychotic woman is not going to hurt my sister."

"I'm doing everything I can to keep my family safe and make no mistake about it, Brynley is part of my family. But, things may be dicey around here for a while. I don't know how long you plan to stay, but it might be better if you kept your distance."

"No freakin' way. If Bryn is in danger, I'm not leaving."

"If Brynley was my sister, I'd feel the same way."

Lavina raises an eyebrow. "If Brynley was your sister, this whole conversation would be wildly inappropriate."

"Touché. Anyway, I can understand why you want to stick around. I just needed to tell you the real score."

"What are you going to do about Kara-Jane?"

"I wish I knew."

"You better figure it out. From what I can tell, Kara-Jane isn't going to gracefully bow out of your life just because you fell in love with my sister."

"I know. Isn't it ironic? For years, I prayed that she would come back. Now, I hope she goes away and stays gone."

"I hope she does because you're the kind of man my sister deserves."

"Thanks for the vote of confidence."

"No sweat. So, I gotta ask you a question. Is Mindy Whitaker as cool as she seems?"

"Nope." I grin at Lavina's crestfallen expression. "She's even cooler."

"Really?" Lavina asks with a hopeful expression.

I hold up my injured arm. "Really, really. I'm not up to playing just yet. My friend Declan is covering for me. They have a gig in Eugene this weekend. Would you like to go?"

Lavina's face lights up. "Does it rain in Oregon?"

I smile when I see Brynley and Brody walk across the restaurant toward us. Brody is clutching a stuffed animal. Obviously, Brynley has been hitting the claw machine again.

Brynley stops to study her sister. "You must've told her," she guesses.

"I can see why you love this guy, he is way cooler than Manfri."

"Without a doubt. Is everything okay here?"

Brynley asks as she sits down.

Lavina smiles. "Maybe it's not perfect at this moment, but I'm sure it will be soon."

CHAPTER TWENTY-FOUR

BRYNLEY

THERE ARE HEARTS EVERYWHERE I look as Joe and I stroll through the mall. It's funny, I used to believe that Valentine's Day was a made-up holiday designed to torture single people everywhere. Now that I have a phenomenal guy in my life, it feels entirely different. I say a silent prayer of thanks for random encounters.

Up ahead, Brody and Lavina stop in front of a candy store. Brody signs, "Chocolate apple?"

Our new security guard, Beckett signs back, "I don't know, ask Brynley."

Brody turns toward Joe and me and signs, "Mom, apple have?"

It still takes my breath away when he calls me Mom. At first, he only called me by my name sign. However, recently, that has morphed into Mom. He is looking at me impatiently and it occurs to me I should probably answer him. "I dunno, we haven't had dinner yet. Maybe you should wait until after you eat."

Lavina chortles, "OMG! When did you turn into our mom?"

As I think back over what I just said, I hide my face behind my hand. "Holy moly! I have no idea why her voice just came out of my mouth! It's like I'm possessed or something."

Joe snickers at me. "I remember the first time that happened to me. I had been up really late the night before playing a gig. Brody was really whiny and I turned to him and said, "I can give you a reason to cry," as I pointed to his timeout chair. I was horrified. I swore that would never happen."

Brody stamps his foot to get our attention. "Yes or no?" he signs.

Beckett places his hand on Brody's shoulder before he signs, "Be patient."

I grin at the bodyguard. "As much as it is a pain to have you shadowing our every move, you've been really great for Brody's signing skills."

Beckett shrugs. "My parents are deaf. I grew up signing for them. So, this job is a natural fit. I like it here. My last client was the daughter of a billionaire who couldn't stay where she was supposed to be."

Brody taps his foot impatiently and points at the display in the window of the candy store.

I glance up at Joe. "What you think? He's already had his weight in popcorn at the movie. At least an apple would be real fruit."

Joe takes Brody by the hand and leads him into the candy store. "Makes perfect sense to me. After all, it's Brody's birthday. Candy apples for everyone!" he announces with a grin.

A few minutes later, we emerge from the store. Brody's candy monstrosity complete with "dirt" and gummy worms is so large Lavina has to carry it.

After we sit down at a picnic table, Lavina takes a large bite of her chocolate-covered apple. "I gotta say, this is even better than chocolate cake."

Brody grins and takes a gummy bear off his apple and pops it in his mouth.

"I agree, this is a great idea," Joe says.

From behind me, I hear a voice I'll never forget. "Oh look! My man has found himself another whore. This one looks like jailbait."

Beckett adopts a defensive posture.

"Get Brody and the women out of here," Joe growls at his bodyguard.

"I'm staying put," I announce stubbornly. "Apparently, Kara-Jane and I need to have a conversation."

"I got nothing to say to you, you stupid man-stealing gypsy," Kara-Jane snaps.

"That's enough from you," Joe bellows.

Out of the corner of my eye, I see Beckett escorting Brody and Lavina from the food court. My heart breaks when I see Brody asking him who the scary woman is.

"What's wrong, Joe? One girlfriend not enough for you?"

Joe just shakes his head in disgust. "That's rich coming from you. I told you months ago to go away. We've got nothing to talk about."

"What about Brody? He's mine too, you know. I don't want him around this woman," Kara-Jane says as she points to me.

"Okay, first of all, I'm not 'this woman'. My name is Brynley. The other woman you're so worried about? She's my sister. We took Brody to a movie for his birthday."

"Yeah, I know it's my son's birthday. I was there when he was born, remember?"

Joe goes toe to toe with Kara-Jane. "It's convenient that you finally remember Brody's birthday after I've fallen in love with another woman. You might have been there when Brody was born, but you gave up your parental rights a couple years ago. Funny how you forgot that."

"You can't love her! She's awful! I read all about her and how she is scamming you. Have you seen the pictures of her abusing Brody?"

At this point, I stand up. "Look, I don't know how you got those pictures and gave them to the tabloids. But, since you were there, you know I didn't do anything to hurt Brody. He fell off the merry-go-round. Exposing Brody to the media was a dirty, rotten thing to do."

"Well, somebody had to tell the world what was really going on. Joe Summers is not as perfect as he makes himself out to be," Kara-Jane huffs.

I have had enough. I stride over to Kara-Jane and get in her face. "No one ever said Joe is perfect. But you had your chance to have the perfect family and you gave it up. I'm not that stupid. I love Joe and Brody and I'm never going to take that for granted. I don't know what your issue is, but if Joe asked you to leave, do it. He has enough going on in his life without having to mess with you."

Before I can blink, Kara-Jane pulls a bright purple gun out of her purse and points it at Joe and me. Honestly, I want to laugh out loud. It looks like a squirt gun. I glance over at Joe in disbelief. He is taking the situation a lot more seriously than me as his hands are up in the air.

"Kara-Jane, what are you doing? Put that down!" Joe barks.

"No! If I can't have my family, she can't have it either."

Kara-Jane waves the gun around. My heart drops when I realize the word Ruger is stamped on the side of the gun. This deranged chick isn't kidding.

Before I can formulate a response, a blur of motion comes from my left and suddenly, Kara-Jane is on the ground with Beckett's knee in the middle of her back.

Joe goes over to retrieve the gun, which flew from her hand when Beckett took her down.

"Holy crap!" Lavina exclaims. "Did that really just happen? That was like a scene from a soap opera."

Beckett looks up. "Yeah, it's real all right. Somebody might want to call the police or something."

My hands are shaking as I grab for my phone in my purse. Someone else in the food court steps forward. "I'm on it. They're on their way."

I stare at the stranger blankly.

Joe takes a napkin from the dispenser and places it on the table beside me. He gingerly places the bright purple gun on it. Nodding toward Brody he says and signs. "Don't touch. This is real."

Brody runs over and hugs Joe's leg. Tearfully, he looks up and signs, "Why?"

I squat down and hug Brody as he clings to Joe's leg. "That's a really good question, bud. Maybe someday we'll know the answer."

CHAPTER TWENTY-FIVE

JOE

BRODY CRIED THIS MORNING when I dropped him off at kindergarten. He didn't even do that on his first day of school. He kept signing that he was afraid that girl monsters were going to get me while he was away. It took me a while to move from loving Kara-Jane to strongly disliking her, but now I hate her for disrupting my child's view of the world as a safe place. I told him that the bad woman was in jail and that Beckett was here to save me like Superman. Still, he's terrified every time we leave the house.

I try to focus on the physical therapy exercises designed to help me increase my range of motion in my hand. It's hard not to hate Kara-Jane for this too. If I hadn't been going on some stupid fool's mission with her, I would've never been in the accident which may cost me my career.

I jump when I hear the front door open. I gave Beckett the morning off since I'm not planning to go anywhere, so I know it's not him. Cautiously, I get up and look. This mess with Kara-Jane has affected me too.

I'm surprised when I come face-to-face with Brynley. I have to reach out and steady her. It's then I notice she's white as a ghost.

"What's wrong?" I ask as I gather her up in an embrace.

She gives a silent sob. I can feel her shoulders shaking.

"Someone showed my mom and dad all the tabloid garbage. They called me while I was at work. They're demanding that Lavina comes home."

"Sweetheart, they can demand that all they want. But Lavina is over eighteen and has a job."

"I know. Isn't it sweet that Mariam hired her to help with Will's charity until she starts her classes at Oregon State? But Mom and Dad said they wouldn't fill out her financial aid forms for school unless she comes back home. All she's ever wanted was to be a lawyer. I remember when she was little, she used to pretend she was a judge. I feel like I've screwed all that up for her."

I pull Brynley away from me and wipe her tears away with the pads of my thumbs. It causes me to wince in pain, but at least I'm out of the stupid cast.

"You didn't do anything wrong. I know Lavina is thrilled the two of you are reunited."

"But what if her relationship with me costs her everything? I'm not in a position to help her, I'm going to be buried in student loan debt of my own."

I kiss Brynley's forehead. "Bryn, don't worry about it. Lavina is your family and that makes her my family too. I take care of my own."

"Really?" Brynley asks as if she's afraid to be hopeful.

"Really. Since I can't play, I have been writing music

like crazy. Aidan likes my new stuff and is going to produce an album of songs I've written. Things are good."

Brynley hangs her head. "They may not be so good after all."

"Why do you say that? I'll help Lavina go to school. It's not a big deal."

"I can't thank you enough for taking care of my sister, but that's not what this is about."

"What do you mean?"

"I wasn't snooping, I swear. I was trying to track down a mother who is struggling with drugs and didn't show up to her visitation. So, I was looking in local jails to see if she'd been picked up on a drug charge. That's when I discovered Kara-Jane was released this morning."

"How in the heck did she do that?"

"I don't know. But I figured you probably wanted to know to protect Brody."

Brynley pulls her cell phone out of her pocket and checks the time. "I gotta go back to work. I just wanted to tell you in person."

I pull her in close for another hug. "Try not to worry. I'll do everything in my power to protect you and Brody. The last time was too close for my comfort."

Brynley nods. "Mine too. Honestly, I'm scared to death. Kara-Jane should be behind bars. With all due respect, your ex is more than just a little unbalanced."

"I don't disagree," I respond as I give Brynley one last kiss. "Stay safe. I'll work on it, I promise."

<hr />

I flip my address book around in my hand several times

before deciding to make the call I know I must make. Finally, I take a deep breath and dial the number I used to know by heart.

"You've reached Billy John Lovejoy. If you want us to do a gig, please leave your name and number. Otherwise, I'm sleeping, so leave me alone."

I'm paralyzed with indecision as I wrestle with what I should do next. Billy John's phone makes a beeping sound. "Umm, hi, BJ. This is Joe Summers, I just need to —"

"Joey, buddy! Don't mind me, I just answer the phone that way to screen spam calls. What's up?"

I shift the phone in my hand. "It's been a long time, but I need to talk to you about Kara-Jane."

"Oh boy, she's a piece of work. Why didn't you warn me?"

"If I'd known you were going to run away with my wife, I might've said something," I reply sardonically.

"Fair enough. You're welcome to have her back, though. She's nuts."

"That's what I'm calling you about — "

"What did Kara do this time? She have anything to do with your sudden popularity with the tabloids?"

"Pretty much everything. She has been feeding them wild stories and has a pathological dislike of my girlfriend."

"Oh, sucks to be you. But like they say, there is no such thing as bad publicity."

"If it was only the rag magazines, I might just let it go. But she pulled a .380 pistol on my family."

"Geez, I hope she's in jail! Why would she do that? Haven't you guys been over forever?"

"We have been. But when she split from you, she became obsessed with me."

"Funny, she used to feel that way about me and then she met a winemaker she thinks is sexier than me. I guess my dad bod doesn't do it for her anymore."

"I'm not sure what's wrong with her, but she isn't in jail anymore. She got out. I thought maybe you paid her bail or something."

"After what she did to me and the girls? Fat chance. She tried to destroy my reputation at every gig we've worked in the last four years. Then she told the girls' daycare provider I was doing something hinky with them."

"BJ, I'm so sorry. You don't deserve that."

"You never deserved what KJ and I did to you either. I can't tell you how sorry I am we screwed you over. So, how do we stop her from hurting anyone else?"

"I think we have to team up like we used to in the old days. How do you feel about coming to Oregon?"

"It depends. Can we jam while I'm there? I miss playing with you."

I cringe. "I'm not up to playing much these days, but maybe we can write some songs — you know, country songs about our crazy ex?"

Billy John laughs. "That, I can do."

Chapter Twenty-Six

Brynley

THE MICROPHONE PACK DIGS into my back as I try not to fidget on the couch.

I look over at Mallory and Madison as a technician adjusts the position of my microphone. "Are you guys sure this is a good idea? I'm not sure we should antagonize Kara-Jane. She was more than a little unhinged the last time we came face-to-face. Won't this just make things worse?"

Mallory shrugs. "It might. However, Joe's ex-wife didn't show up at her arraignment. Having her out in the wind is not safe either. Hopefully, Madison and I will be able to smoke her out while helping to set the record straight."

Billy John nods his head. "Yeah, it's about time for someone else to set the agenda. If it encourages her to come out of the woodwork, it's a win-win."

"I'm worried she might come after Brody — especially after she discovers we are all working together."

Joe reaches out and grabs my hand. "We've got that covered. Jameson and Tristan assigned extra protection to Olivia, Isabella, and Brody."

Madison sits down on the couch. "Joe, are the kids getting along okay?"

Joe nods. "Brody is really protective of them. It's kind of sweet."

"That's wonderful to hear. Mallory and I are going to ask you some questions designed to elicit the real story about Kara-Jane. If there's ever a question you don't want to answer, just put your hand on your lap and we'll move on to other topics. I urge you to stick only to the facts you know."

Billy John winces. "Yeah, it'd suck if she sued us for defamation or something. I've got enough problems trying to rebuild my career without complicating things."

"We'll do everything in our power to prevent that from happening. I have spent several days verifying background material."

"It's not very often I get a chance to set the record straight in an environment where I'll be taken seriously," Howard adds.

"Howard, thank you for your source material on this story. It was really eye-opening."

Howard blushes. "I keep trying to tell people I'm a good guy. But then they find out what I do for a living and everything changes."

Just then, a voice from offstage says, "Live in five, four, three, two, one!"

Madison smiles toward the camera. "Hello and welcome to *This is Life with Madison*, I am Madison Black. I am honored to have Mallory Yoshida here from *Word Soup, PNW*. Mallory is an award-winning investigative reporter. She's here with my friends Billy John Lovejoy, Howard Keely, Brynley Meeker and, of course, our very own Joe Summers. Today we'll be talking about the downside of being a public figure when your relationship crumbles. We'll talk about when cyberstalking becomes all too real. As you may know, I have several rather famous friends. Recently, I've seen their reputations be destroyed. Mallory, can you give our audience some idea about the scale of the problem?"

Mallory sits forward a bit on the couch. "You know, it's hard to get exact figures on this phenomenon. Social media, blog sites, and tabloid television shows and magazines have become so accessible to people. Very few of these stories are actually vetted properly. Unfortunately, it has become far too easy for people to destroy each other. For example, in a recent study it is estimated that over ten million Americans have been the victim of revenge porn."

Billy John breathes out a sigh of relief. "Boy, it's a good thing I'm shy. Otherwise, I'd be in a world of hurt."

"Sometimes it doesn't matter how shy you are. Many of these pictures are taken without consent. Anyway, I'd like to hear from Joe about how all of this started for you."

Joe shifts uncomfortably on the couch as he starts to tell his story. "Kara-Jane and I met in high school. I was instantly smitten. She came from a rough home environment, so we got married right out of high school. I thought I could fix everything for her. First, she was really supportive of my music career. I tried to focus on that and make a go of it in the beginning, but it was obvious I wouldn't be able to support her on just my music alone. Besides, before my mom passed away, I promised to become a teacher like she was before she got sick. Anyway, I was busy trying to juggle school and my songwriting career."

"Sounds like a real challenge," Madison comments.

"It was. And then it got even more complicated when, after a few years of barely scraping by, Kara-Jane got pregnant with our son. Even though I was crazy busy, I was excited to be a dad. I don't have any family left, so Brody was a miracle to me. Kara-Jane was told as a teenager, she would not be able to have children. So, this was unexpected, to say the least."

Madison grins. "I know all about unexpected pregnancies. They can throw you for a loop. So, what happened next?"

"I was shocked Kara-Jane didn't really take to motherhood. She only cared for Brody if there was no other option. In fact, there was one time she totaled my van I used for music gigs with Brody inside. She didn't even bother to take him to the doctor. I was out of town that weekend performing a gig up the coast of Florida and never even knew Brody was injured until I got back."

"Oh no!" Madison exclaims. "Was Brody okay?"

Joe nods. "As far as I could tell. But I didn't have much time to dwell on it because the next thing I knew, she was packing up her stuff and taking off with this guy."

"Wow! Yet you're here today together. That has to be a difficult thing." Madison comments. She looks over at Billy John. "Can you tell us what happened next?"

Billy John scrubs his hand down his face. "This is hard for me to admit because Joe Summers used to be one of my best friends. Then I betrayed him and everything our friendship stood for. So, this is my public apology to my former best friend. I'm sorry."

Joe reaches out to shake Billy John's hand. "I appreciate that. I guess I've always had one question for you – why?"

Looking sheepish, Billy John clears his throat. "That's a really good question. I guess back then, I had a really strong hero complex. After your son was born, Kara-Jane started flirting with me. At first, I just ignored it and after a while, she started adding horrific details about how you were physically and emotionally abusing her."

I gasp and cover my mouth at the revelation. My eyes fly to Joe for an explanation.

His jaw sets and he glares at Billy John. "BJ, we were friends for years. You know that's not true! Why didn't you just ask me for the truth?"

"Honestly, she had me so twisted up I didn't know which way was up. She had me convinced that if I said anything to you that you would punish her. Finally, I decided the only way to keep her safe was to take her to another continent."

Joe looks like Billy John kicked him in the gut. "You were my best friend. How could you even think I would lay a hand on Kara-Jane? Back then, I thought the sun and moon rose at her command."

Billy John sighs. "I dunno. I guess love makes you do crazy things. Karma bit me in the butt, though. Things were great in the beginning. Kara-Jane was helping me book gigs and helped me find new bandmates. We had a great time traipsing across Europe. Then, Kara-Jane got pregnant with the girls. I was naïve and bought her story when she told me she had her tubes tied after your son was born. Now, I'm the proud dad of two preschool girls. Girls she told me weren't in the cards for us. The timing sucks, but I'll never regret them."

Madison nods. "So I take it since you're speaking

with us today, your relationship with Kara-Jane didn't end in happily ever after?"

"Far from it. I mean, I was trying to keep it together and then she started going on all these wine tastings with her girlfriends. Thank goodness for my parents because she didn't even care if I had to work. She would just take off and leave the girls to fend for themselves."

"I don't even have kids yet and I can't imagine doing something like that," Mallory comments.

Joe shrugs. "I can't either. Being a parent is the best thing that's ever happened to me. But it appears my former wife doesn't care much for being a mother. That's why I was shocked when Kara-Jane popped up in my life again."

"What do you mean?" Madison asks.

"I don't remember this because some driver who was texting T-boned my car and I ended up in the hospital with a head injury and my hand mangled — but when Kara-Jane tracked me down in the hospital, she swore I had agreed to meet with her. Even though I was completely beat up and in great pain, Kara-Jane insisted I should take her back and support her new pregnancy — which incidentally I didn't have anything to do with since I haven't slept with my former wife in almost five years. When I refused, she threatened to ruin my reputation."

I elbow Joe. "Don't forget she almost destroyed our relationship. She made it sound like you had promised to take her back. Until my friends talked some sense into me, I believed her."

Joe brushes some hair behind my ear. "Yeah, I wish I could forget about that part too. But, that wasn't the worst of it —"

Howard clears his throat. "Before you get to that

part, maybe I should explain what happened behind the scenes."

Madison turns toward the camera. "For those of you who don't recognize Howard Keeley, he is a senior reporter for *Scoops & Icons*. Although technically his paper is focused on lightweight stories, he is one of the most ethical members of the paparazzi community."

Howard blushes. "Thank you, Miss Madison. You make me sound downright respectable even though I work for a gossip magazine. Even though tabloid magazines are known for running salacious stories, I have standards. I was shocked when someone was shopping around wild stories and compromising pictures of Mr. Summers. You see, Mr. Summers plays in the same band as my niece, Tasha. Over the years, I got to know the performers with Silent Beats pretty well. I knew the stories couldn't possibly be true. So, I took a hard pass." He cringes. "Unfortunately, my colleagues at less reputable papers did not. So, I had to sit on the sidelines and watch a friend's reputation be butchered. I've never been so ashamed of my profession."

Mallory leans forward. "Howard, you've been in the business a long time. Have you noticed a change in the stories you are offered?"

"Oh yes, ma'am. Most certainly. After my brother died of cancer, I left the world of sports reporting to keep an eye out on my young niece, who was part of the pageant circuit. She became estranged from my side of the family when my brother got sick and I knew my brother would want me to watch out for her. So, I started picking up freelance work to pay the bills. Way back then, most of the stories we ran were about stars who got in trouble with the law or had a beef with someone on their set. We ran a lot of stories about UFO sightings and silly stuff like that. The coverage is definitely more personal now. It seems like everyone is bent on destroying someone else. It makes me sad."

"I imagine so," Madison remarks. "Having been the target of some of these articles, I'm well aware of how personal things have become. So, when you were presented with all those negative stories about Joe and Brynley, what did you do?"

Howard leans forward and adjusts his tie. "Well, I tried to just turn them down and put them out of my mind. You know, I am pitched story ideas all the time that I don't use. After a while, I started thinking about how it would feel if these stories were about my niece. Then, I decided someone should investigate why this was happening to Joe. So, I called Mallory here because I know she's a top-notch investigative reporter."

Madison shifts on the couch to face Mallory. "Without going into the specifics of how your paper investigates the background on your stories, can you tell me if any of the charges of spousal abuse or child abuse were ever verified?"

Mallory shakes her head. "Not only were they not verified, they were completely debunked by Joe Summers' employers, coworkers and childcare workers. The same is true of Joe's girlfriend, Brynley Meeker. She is an exceptional student who worked her way through college and is about to get her Master's degree in social work. As nearly as we can tell, this was a malicious planting of untrue stories to damage their reputations. Incidentally, our investigation showed that Billy John is also a well-respected parent who works very hard to provide for his family."

Madison leans forward and asks, "Did you ever

contact Kara-Jane about the inaccuracies in her stories?"

Much to her credit, Mallory simply nods. "We did. She denied them, of course. We had evidence to disprove every allegation she made, but she screamed into the phone. "It doesn't matter what you think, I'll fix this for good."

I raise my hand slightly. "I think I can pick up the story from here. Our next encounter with Joe's ex-wife occurred in front of his son on his birthday. Fortunately, we have a very talented bodyguard who prevented this situation from getting much worse."

"Worse?" Madison asks.

I nod. "Kara-Jane started the encounter by insulting me, my sister, and Joe. I was not having any of that. So, when I pushed back, Kara-Jane pulled out a .380 Ruger pistol. I knew exactly what it was. My dad is a gun guy. So, despite the fact that it was bright purple, it didn't take me long to figure out it was real."

"My heavens! What happened then?" Madison asks, looking genuinely shocked.

"Initially, our bodyguard was getting Joe's son out of earshot from her insults. However, when she pulled a gun, he tackled her to the ground until she was arrested by the police."

"Sounds like you're safer with her in jail," Madison replies.

Joe's lips form a tight line before he adds, "We would be if my former wife was still in jail. Unfortunately, she was able to come up with bail money before her formal arraignment."

Madison's eyes widen. "So, you're telling me that Kara-Jane Lovejoy not only made up allegations against you, your best friend and your girlfriend, she tried to shoot you as well?"

"Exactly," Joe sighs. He holds up his injured arm and shows the audience his cast. "I've now had three surgeries to take care of the damage caused by a careless driver. I don't need to worry about how to protect my family from someone who has decided she's out to get me. No one, and by no one, I mean Brynley, her sister, me, or Billy John has done anything to Kara-Jane. Whatever has happened in her life, she brought on herself. I just want her to pay for the crime she's committed and get out of our lives, so we have some peace."

"I understand this whole ordeal must've been incredibly frightening for everyone involved. How is your son?"

Joe looks at me and I shrug. This is his decision. We knew this question might come up. Joe is ambivalent about how much he wants to disclose about Brody since Kara-Jane is still on the loose.

I squeeze his hand in reassurance. Joe swallows hard. "Madison, I'm glad you asked. Brody was certainly frightened by the incident, but it's really hard to figure out how much it affected him. Although he is rapidly learning sign language to communicate, Brody doesn't speak."

"Oh, I'm so sorry," Madison blurts. "Is there anything that can be done?"

"We are very fortunate. Brody is incredibly healthy. He has had many rounds of testing to determine he does not have a hearing impairment. We're not sure what caused his lack of speech — he used to babble as an infant and then that just stopped. The introduction of sign language is helping Brody immensely. Just like parents everywhere, I'm doing the best job I can and Brynley has made it so much easier."

Madison gets a signal from offstage. "I only have time for one more question. Brynley, I know it was hard on you to see Joe attacked. How are you holding up?"

"As awful as all this has been, it's not all bad. The pictures the tabloids printed allowed my sister to find me after several years of being apart. I am grateful. Additionally, the whole ordeal has taught me to stand steadfastly behind the people I love even if you don't know what the future holds. I never expected to find a man with a son and fall instantly in love with both of them. So, Kara-Jane may think that her antics are going to drive us apart and Joe into her arms again. I'm here to tell you that's never, ever going to happen. I love Joe and Brody with my whole heart. I'll be here until they tell me to leave."

Madison dabbed at her eyes with a Kleenex. "You know I love a great love story. I hope our viewers can help find Kara-Jane so you can feel safe again. I know how scary it is to have someone after you, but I believe the viewers will help make sure Brody's family is strong and safe. Thank you so much for sharing your story." Madison looks directly at the camera and says, "After this brief commercial break, we'll be discussing the best way to travel during spring break."

The stage manager makes a hand signal and the cameras turn off. Madison stands up and hugs each of us. "Thank you for sharing the whole story. Maybe someone will find Kara-Jane and she'll be locked up like she should be. I hope the fact that you're fighting back will discourage someone else from lashing out at someone they love."

"Thank you for giving us this opportunity," I say as

I stand there clutching Joe's hand. "It means a lot to us to set the record straight."

"I hope Mallory and Howard's efforts pay off. You guys have had enough pain in your lives. You deserve your happily ever after."

JOE

I enter the kitchen with Brody on my shoulders. "Okay, I've done enough of the heavy lifting. Go wash your hands so we can have dinner. I'm going to pop this pizza in the oven." I set Brody down and he runs off toward his room. After he leaves, I yell out toward the living room where I can hear Brynley typing on her computer. "Hey, I got your favorite kind this time and I even bought tomatoes. You should be proud of us. We were two men on our own and we got vegetables on pizza," I explain with a good-natured grin. "I can't believe how refined you've made us. Pretty soon, we'll have to start using salad forks."

Brynley looks busy, so I start putting groceries away. Eventually, I wander over and kiss the back of her neck as she reads something intently. "What are you doing? Tough case at work?"

Startled, she looks up. "Did you get this email from Madison?"

"I dunno. I was laying down tracks with Mindy and Tasha today. I didn't even have time to look at my phone."

Brynley balances her laptop on her knees as she points to the screen. "You may want to read this. It's about Brody. Madison forwarded it to me. It's from a specialist in speech disorders. I did a little research and it seems like this guy might be on to something."

"Why would a specialist send an email to Madison?"

"Remember when we were on her show a couple weeks ago? You were talking about Brody and how he lost his speech. This guy is a doctor and he has an idea about why he doesn't talk. I googled everything and even though I'm not a doctor, it seems really plausible."

It's a good thing I'm standing behind Brynley and she can't see me roll my eyes. "Oh goody … another specialist. You know, because I've had so much luck with them before."

"I know you don't trust doctors much, but please just read this. It explains everything. When I first met you, I figured maybe Brody was on the autism spectrum. But as he learns more sign language, he doesn't rock up on his toes anymore. I think that was a mechanism to cope with his frustration about not being able to express his needs."

Reluctantly, I go over and flop down on the couch. I place her knees over my legs and motion for her to hand me the laptop.

Brynley watches me anxiously as I read, reread and read the email from the doctor again. After several minutes, she whispers, "Well, what do you think?"

My hands feel numb and I have to remind myself to breathe. "Holy —"

"I know, right? I'm just dumbfounded. Neurogenic

muteness could be the answer. Brody was injured in a car accident around the time he lost his speech, right?"

"Brody stopped talking right about the time Kara-Jane left. That's why some of the doctors thought he just voluntarily stopped talking. But what if they're wrong and it's because of the car accident. I never even thought to mention it. It was several hours after the accident before I got home to take him to the doctor. The ER said they didn't find any significant injury. What if we missed something?"

Brynley points to the laptop. "Now, you have a place to start looking for answers. You can stop beating yourself up. If this doctor is right, you didn't have anything to do with the reason Brody can't speak."

I set the computer on the coffee table and lean over to hug Brynley. "I owe you so much. Your friends came through for me in a big way. Even if we haven't found Kara-Jane yet, we've still won. You gave me the courage to be honest about what was going on even though it's hard for me to talk about."

"If I had my way, the world would be perfect for you and Brody. But, you're forgetting something — these are your friends too."

I hug her closer. "That's true. But before you came into my life, I was too busy proving to the world I can handle it all on my own. You taught me that it's okay to not be perfect and ask for help."

<hr>

I knock on the door frame outside of Tyler Colton's office. Logan seems to think Ty has good news, I'm not so sure. Whatever it is, he didn't want to give me the news over the phone. To me, that doesn't bode well.

"Hey Joe, thanks for stopping by. I'm sorry I couldn't come to you but I have back to back conference calls today," Ty greets.

I take a deep breath and blow it out before I sit down on the comfortable leather couch. "Let's get this out of the way first. This, whatever it is, doesn't have anything to do with Brody, does it?"

"Yes and no. This will impact him pretty much but not in a negative way. I got word from my contacts in Bradenton that Kara-Jane has been taken into custody."

"Thank goodness. Was anybody hurt?"

"Not to my knowledge."

"What was she doing in Bradenton? That's nowhere near where she and Billy John lived."

"It's still early in the investigation, but I guess she tried to pull a similar number on a winemaker she's been seeing in Florida. He saw an Internet story about the interview you did with Madison. This guy said it all sounded too familiar. So, he called the police. When they located her, she was working as a janitor at a family medicine clinic. When the employer opened her locker, she had several ultrasound pictures and chart notes belonging to patients of the clinic. Her employer is looking at pressing charges as well."

"What was she thinking? I mean, I used to love her once upon a time. I don't recognize the person she's become."

Tyler nods. "I understand. I have a hunch I know what she was doing."

I raise an eyebrow and stare at Tyler.

He consults a pad of paper. "Okay, I'm a little ahead of the evidence here, but if you had told a bunch of people you were pregnant and you really weren't, how would you convince everyone you actually were?"

I rub my temple. "I suppose if I was as evil as my former wife, I might steal someone else's medical records to convince some poor schmuck that he was going to be a daddy."

"Unfortunately, the guy she chose isn't exactly a poor schmuck. He is quite well-off and downright livid she tried to take advantage of him."

"So, what does that mean for us?"

"Oregon will do an extradition dance with Florida and the winner will try her first. Take some time to enjoy yourself before the trials start. I have a feeling there'll be more than a few fireworks."

I reach out to shake his hand. "Thank you so much for your help. For the first time in a very long time, I will sleep soundly tonight."

CHAPTER TWENTY-EIGHT

BRYNLEY

I GRAB MY PURSE and try to run out the door, but it catches on the handle of my office chair, sending it flying across the room. "Shoot!"

Kendall bends down and starts to help me pick things up. "What's wrong?"

"Oh, it's nothing. I'm just totally stressed out between this job and my practicum. I feel like all I ever do is fill out paperwork. I was going to watch some Hallmark movies or something this evening."

"Sounds like a plan. You've been burning a candle at both ends and in the middle. You need a break."

"I thought I was getting one tonight, but Joe keeps texting me about going grocery shopping with Brody. I don't know what that's all about. Maybe he's having a meltdown or something. Since Brody has gotten a handle on sign language, it doesn't happen very often. Oh gosh, I hope he's not getting sick. I don't have time for that."

"Brynley, take a deep breath. It's only grocery shopping. How long can it take?"

I stop what I'm doing and laugh out loud. "You've

never been grocery shopping with a six-year-old, have you? Shopping trips are never quick."

Kendall puts her arm around my shoulders. "I know it's hard, but cherish these moments — even as chaotic as they seem. Trust me, when all the chaos goes away, the silence can ring even louder."

I paste a smile on my face. "Okay, you're right. I am incredibly blessed. Grocery shopping it is. But, if Brody asks for frosted animal crackers, I'm not even going to try to fight."

"Sounds good. Have a good time."

I roll my eyes and head out the door.

⎯⎯⎯⎯◆⎯⎯⎯⎯

Our huge cart is starting to get heavy to push. Brody is stuck on choosing his favorite kind of soup and my head hurts because of the inane music playing over the sound system. I study the list Joe wrote.

"Why is there yogurt on this list? I just bought some a couple days ago. Didn't you find it?"

"Humor me. After all, they have gotten really good at stocking Brody's favorite kind."

Frustrated, I throw the list into the cart. "Okay, but I'm telling you I bought some, and as far as I know, Brody hasn't touched them."

Brody pulls me toward his favorite dairy food aisle and signs, "Strawberry yogurt please?"

"Hold your horses, I'm coming," I say as he drags me down the aisle. "This is weird. The only brand they have in strawberry is Brody's favorite. Usually, we have to sort through all of them to find them."

Brody studies our choices carefully. Suddenly, he

237

reaches in and grabs one. He tries to put it in my hands. "Brody, I know you like yogurt, but we have three more just like that at home that you need to eat."

Brody sits down in the middle of the aisle reminiscent of the first time we met. I squat down and sign, "What's wrong?"

He tries again to hand me the yogurt. "Brynley open please!" he signs insistently.

"Brody, are you hungry? We don't just open things in the middle of the grocery store. We have to pay for them first."

Joe steps forward and places a hand on my forearm. "He is getting upset, why don't you just go ahead and do what he asks? We'll settle up with the store later. It's not like they don't know where we live."

Sighing, I glance down at Brody. "What are you going to eat this with? Your fingers?"

He nods eagerly.

I shake my head in dismay, but I'm just too tired to fight. "You're such a goofball."

Brody holds the yogurt container out for me to open. This is really weird because he usually opens them on his own.

I start to pull the plastic ring off the yogurt, but it's not there. I move to put it back and exchange it for another and Brody shakes his head. "No, I want that one," he signs.

"Brody, the safety seal isn't on this one. We should get a new one."

He shakes his head and signs, "This one!"

I look up at Joe helplessly. He shrugs. "The inner seal is probably still there."

I sigh as I take the plastic lid off the yogurt. Then I gasp when I see what's inside.

In an instant, Joe is on his knee, holding the ring that seconds before had been laying on the clear plastic protecting the yogurt. Brody is holding a sign. I have no idea where he was hiding it, but it says, "Brynley, we love you. Please marry us!"

"You guys are asking me to marry you in the middle of the dairy aisle? Oh my gosh!"

My hands are shaking and I can feel my face heat with embarrassment as other shoppers stop and watch us in stunned silence.

"Brynley Summer Meeker, will you please do me the honor of becoming my wife? You are everything I dreamed of. Before you came into our lives, we were lonely and just getting along. Now, you light up our lives and make us one big happy family. You have captured both my heart and Brody's. We never want you to leave. Please marry us."

I have to blow out a deep breath and draw in another quickly before I can answer, "Why not? I love you too and you are my heart — and according to Will, you guys have always been my heart wish."

Brody lays his hand on my heart and asks, "The heart of Summers?"

"That's one way to put it. My heart belongs to both of you. So, it really is the heart of Summers."

EPILOGUE

JOE

BRYNLEY SMOOTHS OUT AN invisible wrinkle in her skirt. "You didn't tell me all these people were going to be here! You just said it was a get together of my closest friends. There are more people here than were at Will and Mariam's wedding."

I chuckle. "You know this crew. They don't really need an excuse to celebrate, but your hooding ceremony is more than reason enough."

Brynley leans her head back and rests it against the wall. "I can't believe I forgot to bring my cell phone to take pictures. This is only the biggest accomplishment of my life and I don't even have any pictures to post."

I point to the dance floor. "I wouldn't worry about it, Bryn. I think several people have us covered. See, Howard is over there snapping pictures like crazy."

Brynley fiddles with the honors cords around her neck. "Do you think I should wear these here, or is that totally over-the-top ostentatious?"

"You earned those honors cords, wear them with pride. If somebody is intimidated by that, screw them.

You are phenomenal. Sometimes, you worked three jobs while going to school and got nearly straight A's. I am so proud of you!"

"Where are Lavina and Brody?" she asks as she adjusts the bobby pins in her hair. "With the way everyone is hanging around, I'm almost afraid this is another surprise wedding."

I snicker. "If it is, it's a surprise to me too." I gesture in the general direction of the bleachers. "I don't worry about your sister, she can hold her own. In fact, now that Brody is getting better at communication, I worry about him even less."

I scan the crowd looking for Brody and Lavina. It's useless, I'm too far away. I can't see anything but colorful blobs. Just then, like something out of a cartoon, one area of the audience is illuminated. Brynley gasps when she sees familiar silhouettes.

She looks back at me with a flabbergasted expression. "Joe, those are my parents!"

I stop just short of a giggle. "They sure are. Why don't you go say hi?"

She blinks. "You don't understand! They haven't spoken to me in years, yet they are here."

"Go see them. I'll be right here with the rest of our friends, in case you need some reinforcement."

"Reinforcement is an understatement. They haven't said a civil word to me in years. When I tried to get Lavina ready for college, they reaffirmed they never wanted to speak to me again. I figured it would be that way until the day I die. Why are they here?"

"I knew you were sad that they might miss one of the biggest milestones in your life. I set out to change that. I've been talking with them for more than a month.

They miss you so much."

I watch them as they walk over toward Brynley and me. My heart beats faster for Bryn. What do you say to strangers who used to love you?

Brynley's mom quietly gives Brynley a hug while her dad examines his daughter from head to toe. "You're looking good." He picks up her hand and examines the ring. He glances up at me. "Very good. Just enough sparkle for my daughter." He pats his daughter's cheek. "I see you fell in love with a *gadjo*. Do you think I'll actually give my blessing to such a union?"

"I know he seems like an outsider to you, but he's not. I love Joe so much it's like we share a heart."

"Does he understand the Roma are proud people and we have our own traditions to uphold?"

"I do, sir," I answer, interjecting myself into their conversation. "I honor everything your daughter is — including her past, her present, and her future. She is the other half of me I didn't know was missing until we found each other."

Her father looks at her mother and asks, "What do you think?"

"I think the *gadjo* looks at our daughter the way you used to look at me. Even though he is an outsider, your daughter is happy. Who are we to take her joy away?"

Aidan walks up beside me and taps me on the shoulder. "I'll give you guys some time to catch up. My boss needs me for a moment."

"Oh, okay. Becca has Brody, right?"

I nod. "Last I heard they were involved in some elaborate scavenger hunt. Have fun with your family, I'll be back soon."

Aidan and I walk across the dance floor in the bar

Aidan rented out for Brynley's graduation party. Sawdust & Horseshoes has become our favorite hangout. After we are out of earshot, I ask Aidan, "Are you sure about this?"

"I'm positive. You are more than ready to take this step. Brynley is going to love it."

"Whatever you say Bossman."

I grab my favorite guitar and head toward the stage. No one notices when I perch on the metal stool. I tap the microphone stand to get everyone's attention.

"Thank you for coming tonight. I know everyone is proud of Brynley and what she's accomplished. Her heart is amazing and her capacity to give of herself is unmatched. Because of her, my son can communicate in ways we never dreamed of a couple years ago. Brynley stood beside me when I was too sick to advocate for myself. She's nursed me through, not one but two, health scares. She even stood up for me and didn't run for the exits when my former wife tried to shoot her. Most importantly, Bryn loves my son and she understands me well enough to know I'd never be truly happy without music in my life. So, for all you do and all you mean to me, this song is for you, Brynley Summer Meeker. I love you more than I ever dreamed was possible. Like you say, if this is a fairytale, I never want to wake up."

I start to play the introduction to *Thousand Years*. I'm still getting used to playing my guitar with one hand. It's a skill I never thought I'd need, but one I'm grateful to have.

When Brynley hears the opening notes, she looks at me with wide-eyed shock. "How did you know this song is my favorite song of all times?"

I wink at Lavina. "I have secret ways to work my way into your heart."

"I've got news for you, Joe Summers. You've owned my heart since the day you almost passed out in the dairy aisle. I love you too."

Note from the Author

Dear Reader,

Thanks for giving my book a read. If you liked reading about people who are not so stereotypical, then I've got good news …

… there's more.

I have two other series. *Identity of the Heart* is the first book in the Hidden Hearts Series.

Tattoo apprentice artist, Rogue Betancourt has always been a bit of a loner.

Her boss, Marcus Brolin sets out to fix that by signing her up for an online dating service without her knowledge.

Little did he know that that one move would change their lives forever and make everyone question what they thought they knew about themselves.

If you love sweet romance with a hint of mystery,

Mary Crawford

Identity of the Heart is for you.

Get it now.

~Mary

Because love matters, differences don't.

ACKNOWLEDGEMENTS

I've been planning to write about Joe Summers for quite some time. He was first mentioned way back in Hearts of Jade, which is the third book in the Hidden Hearts Series. For some odd reason, Joe's book kept getting pushed aside in my writing schedule as other stories came to the forefront.

Now, I understand why. He was waiting for me to introduce Brynley Meeker. These two didn't have an easy time of it because real life is sometimes messy. However, I hope you loved this unconventional love story as much as I enjoyed writing it. These two are absolutely perfect for each other.

As I'm writing this acknowledgment page, it is the day before Thanksgiving. I have much to be thankful for in my writing career. I have met all sorts of extraordinary people. It is not possible for me to thank every person who has helped me along the way, but I would like to individually thank some people.

First, thank you so much to my beta reader and phenomenal research assistant Kathern Watts. I appreciate your ability to be a world-class sounding board. My stories are stronger because you give me great ideas.

Lisa Lee is a very talented editor. She keeps me honest to the story and helps make sure my stories are internally strong and complete. Thanks for taking my messy words and helping me create beautiful stories.

Speaking of beautiful stories, I need to thank Kathy McGee, from Covers Unbound, for dressing my books in the most amazing covers. They are stunning and I can't even begin to tell you how much I appreciate all you've done for me.

Christina Bergmann, I cannot tell you how much I appreciate your ability to fix the small things to make a strong story even better.

Thank you to my team of beta readers. You are extraordinary. Thank you for being fans and catching all of my mistakes.

Kudos to LJ Redding, who helps make sure people know I actually write books.

As always, my family is amazing. Leonard Crawford, you came up with a heck of a story idea. I hope you like the way I interpreted your plot twists. I can only do what I do because you are always in my corner.

I am thankful for my sons, who remind me what life is about. I love you so much and I'm so proud of both of you.

Lastly, thank you to all my fans who support diverse characters with big personalities, disabilities and character flaws. I love writing stories about people who could be your next-door neighbors. Thank you for allowing that to happen.

About the Author

I have been lucky enough to live my own version of a romance novel. I married the guy who kissed me at summer camp. He told me on the night we met that he was going to marry me and be the father of my children.

Eventually, I stopped giggling when he said it, and we've been married for more than three decades. We have two children. The oldest is a Doctor of Osteopathy. He is across the United States completing his residency, but when he's done, he is going to come back to Oregon and practice Family Medicine. Our youngest son is now tackling high school, where he is an honor student. He is interested in becoming an EMT.

I write full time now. I have published more than thirty books and have several more underway. I volunteer my time to a variety of causes. I have worked as a Civil Rights Attorney and diversity advocate. I spent several years working for various social service agencies before becoming an attorney.

In my spare time, I love to cook, decorate cakes and, of course, I obsessively, compulsively read.

I would be honored if you would take a few moments out of your busy day to check out my website,

MaryCrawfordAuthor.com. While you're there, you can sign up for my newsletter and get a free book. I will be announcing my upcoming books and giving sneak peeks as well as sponsoring giveaways and giving you information about other interesting events.

If you have questions or comments, please E-mail me at Mary@MaryCrawfordAuthor.com or find me on the following social networks:

Facebook:
www.facebook.com/authormarycrawford

Website: MaryCrawfordAuthor.com

Twitter: www.twitter.com/MaryCrawfordAut